On the Rocks

On the Rocks

A LESBIAN LOVE STORY

SUZAN DIGH

SD PUBLISHING

To all those looking for love,
and, to my wife, with whom I have already found it.

I WATCH out the bus windows as it stops at yet another bus stop at the edge of campus to pick up yet another student heading somewhere on this final day of exams for the year. The vibrating hum of the engine fills the air unpleasantly and I can feel the vibrations from the floor, running up through my feet, making the bus journey to my destination physically tangible. My final trip on this route, from this origin, to this destination, will be emphasized by the ending of the physical unpleasantness of this final ride. This feels fitting for the final day of the university school year, for all, and final, final day of university for others, like me.

All done. Complete.

Well, all done except the walk through the auditorium to the front of the podium where the university president will shake my hand with his right hand and hold out my diploma in his left while some student photographer takes our picture and an announcer out of sight off to the right of the podium announces my name and my English degree and my distinction to the audience of families and friends. Well. To the audience for those who have families and friends. I won't have either in the audience. My family has unofficially disowned me, and my friends, I guess, are really only acquaintances.

"Liz? Liz, are you done exams now?" One of my male class-mates plops sideways into the bus seat in front of me and rests his arm along the back of the seat while he interrupts my staring out the window — my imagining of my graduation ceremony.

I want to say, "Everyone is done with exams now. Exams are over for the semester."

No, what I want to say is actually, "Turn around and leave me in quiet thought while I figure out what I am supposed to do now... next... My path was clear: finish school, graduate university, get a good job, get married, have kids, retire, die..."

But now that I am at the end of university, all I can see is a huge chasm between stage two, finish university, and stage three, find a good job, let alone the whole marry and have kids thing. This is a gap about which I don't feel I was sufficiently forewarned.

I had my head down to complete this degree and to avoid the entire subject of marriage and children, neither of which had ever felt like a stage I would be interested in, nor was it a subject I could discuss with my family.

They have never understood my disinterest in the "normal" future they had envisioned for me, and, even now in the very infrequent visits I make to my family home, they still inquire about when I will find the Mr. Right to fix me up and straighten me out. They have always been convinced that university, and university life, and time in the real world would have sorted me out — helped me move beyond my teenage experimentation.

They have been waiting for me to "outgrow" that phase for a decade now.

I know I need to sit down and have a serious conversation with them, about that, but... I have been so busy with my education and my part-time job, and living whatever kind of life a constantly scrabbling for money, conscientious student who wanted to make the Dean's list, lived. Busy and... well...

The guy — Steve, his name pops into my head — looks at me expectantly.

"Sorry, what did you say? I am still in exam fugue."

He smiles. I think I see a flash of lechery, but then I decide he is just being chatty and I am being overly cynical. "I asked if you wanted to come to the Pool Queue — a bunch of us are meeting there — an end-of-exams blow out. And Thursday they have happy hour pricing."

I don't mention that I am very aware of the happy hours around town. I have been a poor student for nearly five years now. Nobody knows more about happy hours than poor students. Well, maybe poor students and people with drinking problems.

I agree to join him.

* * *

It is not even 4 p.m. when we both get off the bus at the Pool Queue, but, because it is a student hangout with super cheap happy hour pricing, it is not unusual to see it is bustling with young-ish adults, playing pool, or sitting around tables chattering and enjoying the Happy Pitchers of draft beer.

Steve and I join a table of other classmates — former class-mates, to me, now, I remind myself. One of them returns to the table just as I sit, carrying a full pitcher of beer and two clean glasses. He puts the glasses on the table in front of Steve and I. "Ladies first," he slurs a bit — he looks like he has been here for a couple hours already — and proceeds to fill my glass and then the nearly empty glass of the other woman here at our table. He fills Steve's glass, then, after a quick glance at the other three partially empty glasses, tips the pitcher up to his mouth and drinks the remainder in a long swallow, directly from the pitcher.

"Cheers," Steve holds his glass up for clinking while Pitcher Guy is still drinking, "to the end of exams."

I clink against each glass, but not against the pitcher, as it is now empty and Pitcher Guy is navigating his way back to the bar, empty pitcher in hand.

I down my beer in a long swallow too. I don't like beer very much at the best of times, and this is cheap draft, so I drink it like

3

it was intended to be drunk: quickly and completely. This beer is drinkable only because someone else and not my poor student self paid for it.

I slide my chair back from the pub table and stand. I plan to get myself a drink, one I will like more than cheap free draft, but don't offer, or plan, to get any for anyone else. Pitcher Guy might have sufficient funds to pay for draft for six people he barely knows, from a university I'll not be going back to, but that's on him.

Pitcher Guy passes me on his way back with a brand new pitcher. He lifts the pitcher at me and raises his eyebrows, questioning.

"Nope, thanks, I am going to get a proper girl's drink."

He doesn't seem disappointed that I am not going to be drinking more of his beer, though as I watch him walk directly into the back of a chair that was left pulled out from a table and contort himself enough to catch his balance with his non-pitcher holding arm, I am not sure he should be drinking much more of his beer either.

The pitcher is full enough that some does splash out the spout and splatter on the table top. He doesn't stop, however, and the person behind the bar pretends to not have seen this splattering of beer on the table top. The next table occupants will clean it themselves, with their sleeves if they arrive before it dries into a sticky mess, or with the bottoms of the beer mats they'll place under their drinks to keep the sticky off their glasses. Possibly the bartender will wipe down all the tables when he closes, but this is only a possibility, and gauging from the look of some of the table tops, this is not likely to happen.

The bartender has seen me here before. "Long Island?" he asks as he places a tall glass on the bar and turns to the back wall to pick up the vodka and rum bottles, one in each hand.

"Yes sir!" I state with enthusiasm. "I am celebrating. I am done with university."

He nods as he mixes my drink. He is generous with the tequila pouring, and skimpy with the ice, just the way I like my Long Islands.

I don't make chitchat with him, usually, and today is no exception. I take my drink and step away from the bar, intending to head back toward the table of beer drinkers, where Pitcher Guy appears to be emptying his newest pitcher a bit more slowly but still without the pesky interference of a glass, but decide I don't want to rejoin the group at the table.

I move around the edge of the bar, which is set up pretty much in the center of the space, with the tables and chairs and a half dozen pool tables spread around it in various places. It seems haphazard, but, with the bar in the center and the pool tables comfortably spaced, one could lounge here and people watch for many hours, drinking cheap draft — or slightly more expensive but much more alcoholic, Long Island Iced Teas.

I know this for a fact.

There are only four bar stools at the bar. All placed close together but as far away from where the bartender mixes drinks as they could be. This is very intentional. The bartender doesn't want to be engaged in long conversations with drunk patrons. And while I don't know this for a fact, I am reasonably confident that it's true. At least he hasn't engaged in any long conversations with me, over the four years he has worked here.

I select the least sticky-seated stool and set my drink on the bar in front of me. I can see the other side of the room from here, with the table of my classmates behind me.

There are several other groups of people clustered around the tables — I assume many... most... all?... are other students — and spread around close to the pool tables. Some must also be celebrating their final, final exams, but probably more of these are celebrating that it is Thursday, or that it is April, or that they had enough money left after paying rent and bus fare to buy a $8.00 pitcher of cheap draft beer at a pool pub where the price of playing a game of pool is actually more than the cost of a glass of draft.

Along the back wall, almost exactly on the other side of the space from where my own classmates are sitting, are three women playing pool. Well, two of them are playing, the third is leaning against the wall, a drink in her hand, watching.

Watching me, not her companions as they play pool.

I watch back. Time stretches a bit too far. Eye contact stretches a bit too long.

Then I feel uncomfortable and move my eyes back to the women playing pool, as if this was what I was watching all along. I think I can still feel her eyes on me, but I can't bring myself to look up again. I am not fully clear on whether this is because I don't want to see her looking at me, or because I don't want to find out that she is not.

"Another one?" The bartender's voice jolts me. I look at my right hand resting on the bar, holding the glass and its solitary remaining sliver of ice, and nod.

When he returns with my fresh drink and takes away my empty glass, I move back to the table where my classmates have gotten a little louder and a little drunker. Pitcher Guy is slumped in a chair, his eyes half closed and his lips moving, but nobody seems to be able to hear whatever it is he is trying to say.

I sit down with them again and sip my drink. I don't look back toward the three women playing pool, but mainly because I couldn't see them from here even if I did. I try to listen to Steve's argument with one of the other guys at the table — something to do with the student union elections — but don't actually care, for, oh so many reasons... so I just sit here, pretending to listen.

It seems like only minutes pass and my glass is empty, again.

I lean on the table one-handed as I stand. Steve, whose glass is empty, looks up at me expectantly. I had been planning to get myself another drink, but with his expectant look, I change my mind. I have no interest in being expected to buy him a drink. He isn't worth the $8.

"Off to the loo!" And I set my glass, empty save for three slivers of ice this time, firmly on the table. I head toward the bar, past the bar, toward the toilets. As I clear the far side of the bar, I glance toward the three women. The one who had been watching me is playing now, the other two are huddled, leaning on each other, watching the player as she makes her shot. I carry on, into the washroom.

The flush is just finishing its racket and I am zipping my fly when I hear the washroom door open. A woman's voice is speaking in French, quietly enough that I can't make out the words over the noise of the toilet. I step out of the stall and the woman from the pool table is standing directly in front of the stall door, putting her phone into the front pocket of her jeans. The bathroom stall door opens inward, but if it had opened outward, it would have hit her.

"Oh. You startled me."

"Did I? Sorry. That stall," she points her thumb to the only other stall in the room, "— the toilet doesn't work."

I step to my left, toward the sinks, to move out of her way, and she steps to her right, at the same time. We both step back the other direction, at the same time. We both laugh. And I point to my left. "Je vais à gauche."

"Ah, tu parles français?"

"C'est pas ma langue maternelle, mais oui, je le parle."

I move left. She moves with me and scoops her arms on either side of me and stops my movement, and shifts me, gently, backwards so I am pressing against the narrow divider between the two stalls. Her eyes are dark brown and wide open and her lips are full and I can feel the body heat seeping from her.

She kisses me. Her lips pressing firmly, open, I kiss back, tilting my head and allowing her tongue into my mouth. She presses me back against — into — the divider between the stall doors and leans into me. Her mouth is wet and warm and hard and her tongue runs along mine and her breath tastes of rum and sweet. She shifts her body slightly to the side and her hand runs up my hip, slides under my shirt, then over my belly, up my ribcage. Her mouth presses harder, my lips are compressed with the pressure, her tongue dances with mine.

I can't catch my breath. A warm rushing jolt runs down my belly. I slide my hands along her back, up her back, pull her harder against me, as close as she can get with her arm between us and her hand running along my ribcage, against the bathroom stall divider.

Her hand rests under my breast, her thumb brushes over my nipple, hard and quick. Her thigh slips in between mine. I feel myself get wet at the pressure of her thigh, as she presses, rubbing, grinding against me, against the bathroom stall divider.

Then a phone ringing jars me. Well, the phone ringing jars her and she pulls away suddenly, and that sudden change is what jars me. Her hand comes out from under my shirt and her thigh out from between my thighs and a coolness almost immediately replaces her thigh. She steps back and the flush on my face is hot and my lips are cool and wet from her mouth and hot from the blood that flooded them when the pressure of her mouth was lifted. The air is cool on my belly where my shirt is bunched upward and the shape in warmth left by her hand under my breast cools quickly. I brush my shirt back into place and she turns away, toward the bathroom door, her phone coming up to her ear as she turns.

"Oui?" She puts her hand on the door pull but does not open it.

"Ah, Lo, je suis avec des amies," she looks back at me and winks.

I can hear a voice from the phone, quiet and French and female, but too quiet for me to hear what she is saying.

"Tu ne les connais pas... oui, bien sûr. À l'heure... ne te dérange pas. Je t'aime."

I go to the sink and wash my hands. The paper towel is beside her, near the door, so I reach behind her and yank down a sheet, and then a second one. I want to splash cold water on my face — down my shirt — to cool this heat running through me. I watch her in the mirror for a moment, her back is still mostly to me, the female voice on the phone is still talking. She is nodding her head.

As I dry my hands and toss the paper towel into the bin under the sink I hear her say, "D'accord, samedi, à l'hotel, North River. Ok. Bye-bye."

She pulls the door open and waves me through, smiling. "My name is Toni, by the way."

I walk through the door ahead of her and reply, "Liz. Nice to meet you."

One Thursday Night

WE RETURN to her two friends at the pool table, and not to my table of classmates. Barb and Dawn introduce themselves and both shake my hand. Dawn shakes like I am at a job interview. Barb shakes more like my hand is dirty and she doesn't want to touch it. Dawn lives here, in the city. Barb is visiting from Kingston, Ontario. Turns out Toni is also visiting, from Bathurst. They are all staying at Dawn's place and, while they don't specify, it is clear that Barb is probably sharing the bed with Dawn, and Toni... well, she might be sleeping on the couch. I don't ask for clarification.

"Toni's down for the week, been here since Sunday," Dawn informs me as Barb and Toni head off to the bar to get drinks for us all. Rum and colas for everyone. Rum is probably my least favorite hard liquor but, since they are buying, I am not going to be fussy. Or request a Long Island because that might be presumptuous. And they might think I drink a lot.

"Oh yeah?" I respond as nonchalantly as I can.

"Yeah, she has been looking for work, and an apartment too, I guess, but I think she was hoping to find work first. Her girlfriend is coming down on Saturday."

"Oh?" I respond, feeling more interest in this tidbit than I want to express. Not that I am not interested in this tidbit, I just don't want Dawn to know just how interested I might be. Or why.

"Yeah, they're gonna stay at some cheap motel, out past the experimental farm, on the old highway?"

I know where she means. And, I heard the motel name in the bathroom. I don't mention this to Dawn.

"Laurence doesn't have a car, just Toni's, so she's coming down on the bus on Saturday. They have to stay at the motel because I only have the single couch, no pull-out, and no spare bed and... well..." she giggles and looks at Barb as she and Toni return to us, "my own bed is full."

Toni sets a drink on the drink rail on the wall beside us. It is taller than the one she holds in her own hand. "Bartender tells me you drink Long Islands on Thursdays," she smiles.

I pick up the drink and hold it up for cheers, "I do. Happy Thursday!"

We play pool, poorly, for a little while longer, or, possibly, for quite a while longer — it's hard to tell time when the empties all make their ways back to the bar on each refill trip — until the happy hours end and we decide we have had enough pool and cheap drinks and we don't need to be paying the regular price for more of either. The four of us bump our way through the tables to the exit. Toni has driven them all here and her car is in a spot immediately outside the pub doors. When they arrived — sometime late afternoon, but nobody actually recalls what time they got here — there weren't many other cars looking for parking, so they got a prime spot, off street, with no parking meters to feed. Now, the three of them stare at the car.

"Right. Forgot about that part," Dawn giggles, again. Barb snuggles close to Dawn, her arm wrapped around her waist. I look across the parking lot of the grocery store adjacent to the pool pub.

"My apartment is only a few blocks past that store." I gesture toward the store. This is the main reason why this is my favorite pub. Or, one of the main reasons anyway. The happy hour pricing also carries a lot of weight in my rating. I don't mention either of these facts to the trio who are still staring at the parked car.

"Call a cab sweetie," Barb suggests.

"Of course. Don't be stupid. How else would we get home?" Dawn's sharp response makes me look back at them. Dawn has pulled away from Barb and has her phone out. Barb is hugging herself, her arms crossed in front and wrapped around her own midsection. "Jesus," Dawn huffs.

Toni puts a hand in the small of my back and leans close and whispers in my ear, "Where are you headed?"

Dawn is talking to a cab company, her back fully toward us. Barb is looking down at her crossed arms, her head hung and holding herself tightly, as if she is cold and is trying to warm herself up.

It is cool out though, so maybe she is cold. Mid April in New Brunswick, is definitely not a hot spot, but after the long winter, the unusual spring temperature of 8 Celsius at this time of the evening feels pretty balmy. And my face is hot, still... again.

"I just live a couple blocks away..."

"Hmmm... you said. Shall I walk you home?" she asks as her hand in the small of my back slides a bit lower.

"Don't worry about us, fuckers," Dawn blurts. "A cab is coming."

I hadn't been worrying about them. I had only been trying to figure out how to invite Toni home with me, given that I was living in an apartment with a roommate with whom I shared a room. My roommate and I were not lovers, of course, but we both had tight budgets and had been sharing a one bedroom for the past year and a bit. It worked out okay since neither of us had much romantic luck, and, on the rare occasions either of us did, we typically ended up at the other person's place.

I don't have a cell phone. Another thing I just can't afford in my part-time employment and full-time student financial state, so cannot call ahead to warn Chris that I am bringing someone home.

Because I am bringing Toni home with me.

The heat in my groin and the ache just behind my pubic bone is a strong reminder that I have not had a lover in a very long time. A girl's got needs, after all.

As Toni and I head off across the grocery store parking lot, toward my unsuspecting roommate, Dawn and Barb stand stiffly beside each other on the sidewalk in front of the pub, unspeaking, while they wait for a cab.

It takes Toni and I less than 15 minutes — and only one short pause for a deep kiss, which led to one misstep off the sidewalk curb into the street — to walk to my apartment. I turned my ankle just very slightly as I misstepped off the curb, but it does not hurt — it just feels a bit wobbly, like it is overstretched. But Toni puts an arm around my lower back and escorts me the final three or four minutes to home, as extra support. She isn't really supporting me, I don't need that support, but I lean into her as if I do. She is warm and firm and stable.

My apartment building is supposed to be secure, and the front door is supposed to be locked at all times, but it often isn't. Of course, tonight is one of those times when it is locked, so I have to fumble with the keys to let us in. My apartment is in the basement, so we limp down the five steps to the basement hallway. Toni's arm is still around me and our hips bump as we navigate the stairs.

At my apartment door, I knock a short sequence of knocks as I push the door open. "Hi Honey I'm home," I shout into the living space just as we step into it. There is no foyer in this small apartment. "I have company," I add, as the only warning I am able to give my roommate. I hope she is fully dressed. I know she will not be sleeping; she is a night owl.

Chris steps out of the kitchen into the main room. She is wearing a muumuu, which is what she typically wears on those days that she is not required to get dressed in proper clothes, which seems to be most days. She has a coffee cup held in both hands. "Really? Is that what that is?" She tilts her head sideways and peers at Toni, who is now slightly behind me in the doorway.

"Toni, Chris. Chris, Toni." I wave my arm between them.

Chris moves to her recliner, sets the coffee cup on the end table and plops into the seat. She flips the recliner lever and the footrest springs up with a muffled twanging noise. She picks up her coffee cup and sips it while looking over the top of it at us, still standing in the doorway.

"There's no coffee left." She sets her cup down and picks up a novel that she has tucked in a side pocket of a recliner cover she bought online.

Wondering suddenly what I was thinking in bringing Toni back here, I point to the couch. "Ummm... have a seat, I'll find us something to drink."

Toni hesitates in the doorway, not moving.

"Oh, now, this is awkward!" Chris states.

Toni hesitates just another moment before offering a giant polite smile to Chris and then sitting down on the edge of the couch closest to Chris. She sticks out her hand, "Nice to meet you, Chris."

Chris sets her book in her lap and smiles back. "You're a pretty one." She puts her hand into Toni's. I wonder if she just rests it there like a limp princess, or if Chris actually grips Toni's hand.

"Oh. Thanks." A laugh escapes Toni, and she doesn't seem phased at the compliment. I briefly wonder how often she hears that. She is beautiful, with striking features that should catch anyone's eye: short dark brown hair, with deep dark brown chocolate eyes with gorgeous long lashes, and a smile that literally runs from one cheek to the other and shows off strong white straight teeth. Her lips are full and firm and I imagine my own lips are bruised puffy from their insistence.

Toni appears relaxed, clearly at ease in her own skin, and seems comfortable in having a conversation with Chris in what — in a sober state anyway — is a very awkward situation.

My handshake question is answered as I see Chris roll Toni's hand over, palm up. Toni leans in and rests her other hand on Chris's arm as Chris launches into her palm reading explanation.

"Sorry, I didn't exactly plan this... there should be some

bottled water in the fridge at least. Make yourself comfortable," I state needlessly as I head around the corner into our tiny kitchen area.

Rummaging in the near-empty fridge, I find two unopened water bottles and some boxed fruit juices. I take the water bottles. I will not watch Toni sip juice through a tiny straw.

When I return, Chris still has Toni's hand in her own, palm up, and is tracing her finger along the lines in Toni's palm. "And this is your…"

I interrupt Chris. "Chris. Cut out that malarkey."

Both Toni and Chris look up at me. "It's just for fun, Liz, don't be such a crank."

"You're the crank Chris. That stuff is foolishness," I wave the water bottle at their joined hands.

Chris sighs and lets Toni's hand go. "She doesn't like when I read the palms of strangers she brings home in the middle of the night."

Toni laughs, full and loud, and holds out her almost-read palm toward me, for the water bottle. "That happens a lot, does it? I can see why it might be a bit uncomfortable."

I cut Chris a look, "Naw. Chris just likes to be dramatic." I hand Toni the bottle and sit on the couch beside her. Chris has already returned to her book.

Toni opens her own bottle and drinks half of it in one drink. "Thanks," Toni says softly when she finishes. She screws the lid back on and sets the bottle in the crack in the corner where the cushion falls just short of reaching the couch frame, where it remains upright.

I am tempted to correct Chris's insinuation: I have never before brought anyone back here when Chris was home, palm reading aversion or no.

I decide saying something will just make me more uncomfortable, so I don't say anything.

I had left some space between Toni and I on the couch when I sat down next to her. Now she slides her hips closer toward me, closing that space, and puts her arm around my back. She leans toward me and her lips brush my ear. I expect her to speak, to tell me she has to go, that this is just too weird, but she kisses the space just behind my ear lobe, then nibbles the lobe, and I feel her tongue trace along the edge of my ear, moving slowly, lightly, and, interspersed with her exhaled breath, it creates a tingling shiver that sparks some place much lower in my abdomen.

I turn my head toward her and try to connect our mouths, but she leans back, and I am certain I can see a smile in her eyes. Beyond her, I see Chris still sitting in her chair, reading her book.

I close my eyes for a second, wishing I could just open them and be in a different place, a private place, a place where my poverty didn't mean I have to invite people home to share our intimate moments with a roommate sitting unperturbed in a chair right beside us. Or, failing that, a place where I could offer everyone a proper drink and we could all be drunk enough so that I would not have to worry about my roommate sitting in a chair next to us, reading a book while I fool around with my date on the couch.

I place my hand on Toni's thigh, high up, my fingers sliding down between her thighs. I imagine I can feel the warmth coming from her crotch. "Sorry Toni. I wasn't thinking, bringing you back here. I'm a student, and it's been tight the last couple years. And, rents are ridiculous in the city as I'm sure you know. Or you will, once you start looking..."

Toni looks at me curiously, "Oh? Were you talking to Dawn? What did she tell you?"

I wonder if I am supposed to be honest here, or to pretend I don't know that she has a girlfriend coming down on the weekend. "Well. Just that you were down looking for a place. And..."

Chris, who is usually pretty indifferent and doesn't pay much attention to me or, actually, to anything that is going on around her that doesn't involve an opportunity to delve into mystical mumbo-jumbo, has stopped even pretending to read and is obviously listening to us.

Toni finishes my sentence, "And... Laurence is coming down on Saturday."

An uncomfortable silence hangs in the air. Not unexpectedly, Chris doesn't allow it to last very long, "And, who is Laurence?"

Toni flashes her toothy wide smile, but doesn't break eye contact with me. "She's my girlfriend. She's in Bathurst. She's coming down for the weekend, but just for the weekend. She has to work on Monday."

Chris looks pointedly at me. She sets her book aside, attention now fully engaged in the conversation. "So, tell me about Laurence. You two been together long?"

Toni's grin fades a bit. "Going on a year now. Feels like forever sometimes..." She shakes her head ruefully but doesn't speak aloud the sentiment that is clear in her tone: this is not the enjoyable forever, it's a *too long* forever.

Toni squeezes my hand, "It's actually kinda like the opposite of a long distance relationship though. I take some time away, every now and again, to add some distance to our relationship. Sometimes it's hard though, even with the breaks. These weekend visits away are what keep us going. I don't know what it will be like when she moves here."

Chris purses her lips. "Does Laurence... ah, is she aware that you go to pubs, get drunk, and go home with strange women?"

"Chris!" I flush with embarrassment.

Toni just smiles. Her gaze returns to me, roams slowly over my face, down my body. "She knows that I always appreciate what crosses my path. And there's no harm in a little fun, is there?"

I shift, suddenly fidgety. I think more due to Chris's forthrightness than any absent girlfriend. What do I care about some person who isn't even in town. There is something irresistible in Toni, some attraction that, literally, has made me hot and bothered. I can feel the heat emanating from her groin as my hand remains on her thigh, fingers resting in the space between her legs. That same heat radiates from mine. And in the look in her eyes as she continues to gaze into mine.

I find myself captivated by the way her lips curve into a smile and just want to feel them on my own mouth again. I don't want to review what is appropriate in her relationship — what she does with herself is her decision. It's only her who will have to think about the consequences.

I don't need to control this.

I don't want to.

And her hand brushes the top of mine, on her thigh. She squeezes it gently, moving it higher up her thigh, and down, until my hand is fully between her thighs and the edge of my hand is resting against the seam of her jeans crotch.

A jolt runs through me. I don't pull away. The choice I make is partially conscious, partially reckless and almost fully desperate. I need her, and don't care if there is heartache somewhere, for someone, down the road. Just now, right now, there won't be heartache, there will be just pleasure.

Chris breaks the silence musingly, "Guess that's one way to pass the time till she arrives, anyway."

Toni must misunderstand what she sees in my face and she leans back from me and shifts away a little. "Or not. No pressure. I am just out to have a fun evening. It's a short break, and I am just looking to have some fun, nothing deeper — no ulterior motives here."

A weird unease fills me. "I'm sorry Toni, this got super weird."

Toni smiles gently. "It's alright, really... I know, sometimes my situation is a bit much, for people..." She glances over at Chris who is putting her recliner legs down and pauses in whatever she was about to say.

"I'm the one who should be sorry. Liz is right, I'm a crank," she winks at us both, trying to lighten the mood, "but only in my attitude, not in my palm reading. And, now, I will let you two return to... your date. Liz, you can pull the mattress out and that way you won't wake me up, later."

Toni's posture remains reserved but her lips twitch in a hint of a smile, suggesting she appreciates Chris's effort to diffuse the awkwardness. I meet Toni's eyes and shrug. I follow Chris to the bedroom where we have a futon mattress stowed behind the door, for those nights when one or the other of us needs the space to sleep.

"You just met her, Liz. How did you come across such a... well... pretty woman, with such a complex... situation... and take her home to... here."

There is a lot behind Chris's question that I can't answer. And the more sober I become, the more my questions align with Chris's. I don't know why Toni is here with me. I know why I invited her, of course, but not why she would have come, or why she has stayed now that she has seen my living situation.

Now, alone on the small couch together, with the futon on the floor across from the couch, with a single flat sheet and a folded blanket and two flat pillows stacked on one end of it, it seems as though the tension between Toni and I has shifted from that erotic burn to something a little more tense, something almost odd. I make a mental note to make sure I always — always — have some alcohol on hand. Being able to offer my date something other than a bottle of water, or a fruit juice in a box, would probably make this at least a little less awkward.

Toni takes my hand in hers and runs her thumb along the back of my fingers, gently, tickling. Her other hand slips up my back and deftly unhooks my bra.

I feel my blood rushing back to my crotch. As sudden a restart as it was when she pressed me into the bathroom stall divider.

Then her mouth engulfs mine. Her tongue fills my mouth. My tongue fills hers, she slides her hand off mine, slides my zipper down, slips her hand into the now loosened opening and under the top of my underwear, I slide my hips forward to make a less sharp angle, her fingers weave down through my pubic hair, they tickle the top of my slit, just the very top where the curly puffs out.

One finger slides just a bit farther. Into my silken fold. I am so wet even at the very end of my slit, her fingertip slides smoothly, down, up, down, teasing.

She stops suddenly and stands up and pulls me to my feet and pulls my top up — my bra with it — over my head, and pauses with my top over my head and my arms trapped in it and I feel her mouth on my nipple, warm and wet in the cool air, and she holds the top over my head, my arms trapped in its sleeves, while she sucks and nips.

Then she finishes pulling the top off me and presses me toward the futon on the floor and slowly lowers me — us — to the futon with her on top and her mouth on my mouth and biting my neck and my chest and my nipples and my belly and then her hands are on my hips and she tugs my pants and I lift my hips so she can slide them, and my underwear, together, off. She slides up along me and leans on her left arm and pins my right leg under her. Her mouth returns to mine and her fingers walk down my pubic bone and touch my slit again, but lower down and then she slides her finger, her fingers, into me, slow and teasing and slower and more teasing, and then all at once, she just fucks me.

A little while later, as we lie on our backs, our bare legs just touching on the bare futon, the small pile of pillows and blanket and sheet flopped over in disarray on the floor at our feet, both of us completely naked and the scent of our sex on the air, on our hands, Toni's hand pats around and finds me, and she takes my hand in hers. "Maybe next time we could go somewhere a little more... romantic?" She turns her head to face me and I see her lips curl into a soft smile.

I laugh softly, "More romantic than this? Where is such a magical place?" I sit up slowly and the cool air makes me shiver. I grab the blanket and shake it open from a sitting position and drag it over our feet and then lie back down, taking the blanket with me, so we are both covered as we lie there flat on our back on the futon on the living room floor.

My heart races again as Toni's hand runs along the side of my hip and her fingers press into the top of my thigh and I bend my leg to allow her finger to reach my wetness. Her touch, firm and demanding sends electricity through my veins and it feels like only seconds later and she is on top of me, between my thighs, her small pert breasts within reach of my mouth as she leans low above me and we alternate her mouth on my mouth and her breasts in my mouth, while she fucks me again.

* * *

When I wake up, Chris is in the doorway to the living room, holding a cup of coffee in her hand. I tip my head back and look at her, upside down, from my prone position on my back on the futon. Toni is on her side, sleeping, facing away from me. Chris just stands there, looking at us. "Uh, sorry to interrupt." She speaks loudly. Toni stirs. Chris moves to her lounge chair. "It's nearly 10. And I am not hiding in the bedroom all day."

"10!" I jolt upward. "Shit. I work at noon."

Toni sits up too. And stretches her arms overhead.

The blanket is pooled at our feet.

Sipping her coffee, Chris watches us from her lounger as if we were a morning show on TV.

"Chris. Do you mind?" I glare at her as Toni starts to get up off the futon.

"Not too much. I mean, I did when I first came into the room, but now... I don't mind at all." She holds the coffee mug to her mouth and watches Toni pull on her clothing. Toni watches Chris back, smiling as she tugs on her jeans first. She turns to face me as she pulls on her shirt. There is a faded trail of small reddish marks from my teeth running from her neck, down her chest, to the top of her breasts.

Cheeks burning, I don't say anything.

"I feel bad intruding on your space like this. And making things... awkward." Toni is speaking to Chris but has stepped toward me, where I am standing, still fully naked, at the head of the futon. Toni leans in and kisses me deeply. Our mouths taste like each other, and of morning, and, possibly, a hint of stale alcohol at the back of our breath. Then she pulls away and steps

21

back. "And, now, I am going to use the little girl's room and get out of here to let you two get on with your days."

Chris, of course, has seen me naked before, though we both typically sleep in pajamas, but I wrap myself in the still semi-folded sheet while Toni is in the bathroom.

"Well, it looks like you had fun," Chris chuckles.

"But maybe we could find somewhere a bit more private next time?" I continue Chris's thought for her.

"Didn't she say her girlfriend is coming, tomorrow? Not sure there will be a next time, my friend."

And then Toni is back in the living room, looking radiant and not at all like she had just spent the night screwing a stranger on a futon on the floor.

Her charming grin sparks another round of wetness in me. "Laurence doesn't get here until tomorrow afternoon. What time are you done work, Liz?"

"8," I reply.

"I will pick you up. Where?"

I tell her and she kisses me, deep and wet, and waves at Chris and walks out the door.

I rush to get showered and changed for work.

The Week

SOMETIMES I WANT TO HEAR THE LIES

ON WEDNESDAY EVENING Toni is parked directly outside the employee entrance of my work. She is parked so close to the entry that she is nearly blocking the walkway into the store. I would not have been able to miss her, even if I hadn't subconsciously been waiting to see her again. I haven't seen her since I crawled out of her cheap motel bed late Saturday morning, and we did not make plans to meet again. She hadn't even mentioned making any plans. And I wasn't surprised, given that Laurence was arriving within an hour of my crawling out of her girlfriend's bed.

I had been — openly anyway — okay with our two night fling being just that. I figured Toni would pick up Laurence early Saturday afternoon after she saw me off from her motel bed and pretend nothing ever happened the week they were apart.

I did not let my mind dwell on what Toni and Laurence might be doing once they arrived back at their motel room, after a week apart.

But when I see Toni now as I hop into the passenger side of her car, a jolt of excitement spins up through my belly and I wonder how many nights a fling can last before it becomes something else.

"Lo stayed a couple extra days," Toni explains, "or I would have been here on Monday."

"Oh?" I don't have to feign curiosity. I can't imagine why Laurence would have left at all, or why Toni didn't go home with her, or what kind of relationship they must have that Toni could watch me slide out of her bed only hours before her girlfriend likely slid into it.

"Yeah, she helped me with my resume, and wanted to walk through downtown — to sightsee I guess."

"Is she still planning to move here?"

"Yes. When I find a job, and, well, a place — not this place, of course," she laughs as we pull into the cheap weekly rate motel she is staying at, "she is going to move."

She doesn't even ask — and to be fair, she doesn't need to — as we enter the room, she is already tugging my shirt up from my waist. She kicks the door shut behind us and backs me toward the bed, her mouth seeking mine.

The back of my legs bump the edge of the bed and I slowly lower to the bed, Toni holding herself up with her arms as her tongue explores my mouth. My mind still races with questions about her relationship with Laurence while my body responds to her increasingly familiar touch.

I do want to know more, but I fear hearing answers I may not like.

Or do I?

* * *

It's the sound of the shower that finally wakes me up. I look for a clock but the room doesn't seem to have one. The TV remote is on the nightstand on the side of the bed I am on. I reach around the nearly empty Canadian Club bottle and click it. The television blasts on, its volume very high, and shows me an infomercial demo of a super blender mixer combo. I press the up arrow until a channel displays the time: 10:43.

Again... it's late. I have to get to work. I swing my legs over the edge of the bed and hesitantly put my bare feet on the motel room carpet. I imagine I can feel the grime. And then Toni pops out of the bathroom, fully naked and still wet from the shower. "Good morning!" she chirps as she takes the four steps from the bathroom doorway. She stops directly in front of me and leans down and pushes me backward on the bed. I shimmy back so I am lying horizontal across the top of the bed, with my calves and feet hanging over, between Toni's legs.

"Not so fast, ma chérie." She tugs my hips toward her. She straddles me, just above my hips and walks up my body on her knees until my arms are pinned at the shoulders. I bend my knees and shift my shoulders toward her; she moves a little farther and soon my head is pinned between her thighs.

* * *

I have a quick shower and when I come out of the bathroom, Toni has a paper cup of coffee for me on the tiny round kitchen table in front of the window. The curtains are open and I can see her car directly outside it. The TV is still on, but is muted now.

She has her own paper coffee cup and nods at the other chair tucked in at the table, "Breakfast of champions."

I take the coffee but don't sit. "Umm. I actually have to get to work." I feel oddly shy.

"Right. I'll drive you," she grins at me, "but I think you should finish getting dressed first."

I am wearing my pants and socks from yesterday. And nothing else. "Yeah, about that. Any chance you have a top I could borrow. I can't wear the same shirt to work as I went home in last night."

She laughs and nods down at my crotch. "What you got going on down there?"

I would also have liked clean underwear, mine were not in any shape to be worn today. "I am gonna try your commando style." As I say it, a hint of arousal slices through me. There is something hot about knowing Toni's junk is loose in her jeans. But I don't have time for this line of thought.

I drink my coffee. She has spiked it Irish style. I watch as Toni pulls open the drawers in the dresser under the television and finds a shirt that will suit me. When her hands start roaming to check out my commando status, I make her stop assisting me in dressing.

* * *

I take the bus home after work. I had half expected Toni to be there when I exited the store doors. More than half expected, as the sinking feeling in my stomach indicates when I don't see her car in the employee parking area. In the daydreams that got me through the hours at work, with so little sleep and so much anticipation, she had been waiting impatiently outside the employee exit, again.

But she was not.

Chris was not home either. But that was not unusual. Chris has a busy evening life. This is how we made it through so long as roommates in this tiny place: keeping pretty much opposite hours. An apartment time share that worked out most of the time. It was rather uncommon to have our activities collide.

Activities like Toni.

She is on my mind again. Still.

I brew a pot of coffee and pour myself a mug, add a bit of whiskey and settle onto the couch. Music filters through the cheap smart speakers as I sip, eyes closed, soaking in the warmth that spreads down through my chest, and the caffeine. I have picked up a few extra hours at work, now that university is done, but it is not a full-time job.

I have to find a full-time job.

I have to find a career.

I did apply for graduate school, back in the winter, to make the university deadlines. But that was out of habit, or pattern, or... something. Do I want to go to graduate school? Do I want to live like this, like a poor student, for the next 2 years? Or the next six, if I carry on with the doctorate. And, for what?

I envy those people who have a calling. Callings to be fire

fighters or doctors or pilots, or whatever it is. Some people just know what it is they are going to do when they grow up.

I don't even know how to grow up. What does my *grown up* look like? I can't see the house and white picket fence, and there won't be the 2.5 children, and I don't like dogs.

I finish my coffee and make myself another.

I am just finishing the last coffee from the pot when a knock at the door startles me.

Jolts me, actually, I was in some sort of fugue, turning my future over and over and over in my mind.

Opening the door, I'm actually not surprised to find Toni smiling brightly on the other side. "I was hoping I could borrow..." she shakes her head, "hell. Umm... some... sugar? Meh, never-mind." She steps in and puts her arms around my waist and kisses me. Her kiss is wet and tastes like rum.

"Of course, come on in," I reply, stepping back to let her come in.

"No. Why don't you come out. Come out and play!" She giggles, "I'm at the Pool Queue, with Barb and Dawn."

"You been there long?" I ask, even though I know the answer from her giggle, and the way she is gazing at me.

She steps really close and tries to kiss me again, "Or, we can drag out that futon again." Her hand slides down toward the zipper of my jeans.

I am no longer commando, but might have to change my underwear again. I kiss her and our tongues mix in each other's mouths and the tastes of rum and whiskey blend and then she has her hand down the front of my jeans and me pressed against the wall in the living room.

Several minutes later, I am still leaning against the wall, now flushed and breathless.

I meet Toni's eyes and am struck by their intensity. There's an unexpected spark that runs through me and causes a different flutter in my chest.

We walk together back to the Pool Queue.

One drink turns to two, then three as the hours pass in a blur and then, before I know it, last call is announced and we stumble onto the street in a fit of giggles. Toni calls a cab. Dawn and Barb call a cab.

Toni is leaning against me from behind, as we wait. Her lips brush the top of my ear. "Come back to my place. I will make sure you're up in the morning for your early shift."

"She has to!" Dawn blurts, "Laurence is coming tomorrow."

I am surprised at this. "Oh, I thought she only came on the weekends." I had been expecting to go home with Toni tonight, in any case, and tomorrow night too, until Laurence arrived on Saturday. Just like last weekend.

Toni doesn't respond.

Dawn does. "I think Laurence thinks Toni is up to badness."

Toni turns me around and kisses me. Long and deep and full tongue and the warmth spreads down through my belly. And then I don't really care what Laurence knows or doesn't know about Toni's week days.

The cab arrives just then and I get in the back with Toni.

My head is swimming pleasantly.

Her knee rests against mine, and her breath is soft on my cheek as she leans in. Slowly our faces move closer until our lips meet in what starts as a gentle, suitable for the backseat of a cab, kiss. Desire blooms inside me, encouraged by the alcohol, and the temptation of Toni, and, yes, by the thought of Laurence arriving tomorrow and knowing I will have to spend the weekend thinking about Toni with Laurence and wondering if they will be doing this too.

Or not wondering *if* they will be doing this — I think I know that answer — but *how* they will be doing this. Will it be this electric passion that is overwhelming me — with quick screws against the wall, and long ones in a cheap motel, and fondles and deep wet kisses in the backseat of a cab? Or will it be something else, something that you do with girlfriends and not with random strangers you met in a pub bathroom?

Our kiss has expanded now, deepening, and our hands are beginning to explore below the belt.

When we realize the cabbie keeps looking at us in his review mirror, we stop necking in the back seat and shift apart. Toni still holds my hand.

* * *

We just get the motel door open and our clothes start to come off in a flurry, our bodies entwining on the unmade bed. The sheets smell like our sex already... still.

* * *

Toni is passionate. There is no tenderness between us in this round of our drunken coupling. But we fuck well, she is very good at reading my every response. I find myself a bit more aggressive. A bit more reckless, than on previous nights. Toni does not seem to mind.

I would be lying if I don't admit that Laurence passes through my mind once or twice, or that I have a flush, a rush, a thrill every time Toni moans from a bite and I wonder how she will explain these marks to Laurence. But then Toni slides her fingers in me and I stop thinking about Laurence.

I lose myself in sensation.

After, tired and breathless, I lay curled in Toni's arms, her fingertips tracing slow patterns on my back.

"Maid service only comes on Friday," Toni mutters in my hair.

"I see," I reply. And I think I do see. Laurence will have clean sheets when she gets here. That will be a good thing, for Laurence.

Or will it? Should she carry on thinking she's in a relationship with Toni, oblivious to the dozen, or more, times Toni has fucked me here in this bed. Should she just stay in Bathurst... and my thoughts trail off in a haze of tired.

* * *

Daylight is just breaking when I awaken and I am momentarily confused by the unfamiliar surroundings. Then recollection comes flooding back and I turn my head to see Toni still sleeping peacefully beside me. A surge of excitement rips right down to my groin, and then a wave of guilt sweeps back up.

This has been thrilling and time with Toni is... pleasurable, and, clearly, something I had been craving. But the complications are... a lot.

Stirring, Toni smiles sleepily at me. "Morning sexy. Last night was amazing, I'm glad you came back with me." Her words send another rush of butterflies through me and I feel her shift toward me. Her hand touches my hip, starts to stroke, and as the stroking becomes more insistent, more sexual, I put my hand on top of hers. The elephant in the room must be addressed.

"Toni, while I really enjoy this, I... ah. What about Laurence?" I say cautiously.

At this she sits up, running a hand through her bed-flattened hair. "Yeah. Okay. Probably we should have talked about that, her, before now, huh. I should have been upfront from the start — with her, and with you too. Lo and I have been together awhile, we kinda just fell into a relationship. I had just come out, she was experimenting. One thing led to another and voilà, we were a couple."

"Are you in love? Do you love her?" I ask and am oddly fretful about her answer. It should not matter, but it does. For some reason, this answer is important to me. I know I must already know it — if she were in love with Laurence I don't think I would be here in her bed, yet again. Once, drunk, after a night out at a pub is one thing. This... this is something else entirely.

Toni sighs. "I know this is complicated. I guess you could say

30

Laurence and I have an open relationship, so physically we're free. Emotionally though, moving here could change things. I care about you both and don't want to hurt anyone."

I nod slowly, processing her words. An open relationship is new territory for me and I'm unsure how I feel. Part of me thinks it's unfair. Unfair to Laurence and probably unfair to me too.

And then Toni looks at me with her big dark sad eyes and kisses me with her warm firm mouth and presses me back into the flat pillows and slides her naked body over on top of mine. Her tongue plays in my mouth and her fingers move down my body, between our hips, between my legs. And my thoughts of fairness slip away. The world isn't fair anyway.

But before I stop worrying about anything other than Toni's fingers inside me, I force myself to ask, "Does Laurence know about us?" Secretly seeing Toni behind Laurence's back doesn't sit right, but screwing Toni with Laurence's permission also feels somehow wrong. I am not sure what I want to hear as an answer.

She doesn't answer. Her mouth is fully occupied with mine. She releases my mouth as she penetrates me. "Oh, I might be in love. Just not with Laurence."

The thrill that runs through me is as strong as the orgasm.

We spend the rest of the early morning in bed.

"It's okay, I understand," I mumble. And I do. Mostly. Kind of. I understand, I just wish it was different. I wish I didn't have to slip out — sneak out — of this motel room, only to slip back in again, although less sneakily, in a couple days.

Toni is kissing me goodbye outside the closed motel door, while the weekly maid service is inside changing the towels, and the bed, and cleaning the room. As soon as the cab arrives, we will be heading to the Pool Queue where Toni will get her car and head to the bus station to pick up Laurence. I will leave her at the Pool

Queue, walk to my apartment to change, and then make my way to work.

"And I don't envy you this conversation," I murmur against her lips as a cab pulls up beside us and we detach from each other.

We don't talk in the cab, we just hold hands and each of us looks out our own window. I imagine she is planning out her words, how she will break it to Laurence. How she will break it off with Laurence.

I make myself stop trying to figure out what Toni might say, how much she might say, what she will leave unsaid. I just watch the houses go by.

When we get to Toni's car, I hug her and tilt my head for one more long lingering full-mouthed kiss. Toni smiles against my lips. "I will stop by to see you as soon as I can. As soon as I explain to Lo. We'll see where this goes. One thing at a time..."

I nod, and step away so she can get in the car. "I can't wait to see you again." I steal one last glance at her though the open car door before swinging it closed and turning to walk across the grocery store parking lot toward my apartment.

The butterflies in my stomach distract me so effectively that the walk home is a blur. My mind spins with the events of the past week.

Has it really only been a week? It feels so much longer than that.

My routine has been disrupted, first with the ending of my more-than-four years in university and then by this sparking... thing... with Toni that I am powerless to resist. I am powerless to even want to resist. I have no idea what my future should look like. I don't want to even think about my future, to think about plans, and life. I just want to think about the taste of Toni, and the feel of her and the *real*, living-in-the-moment heat and thrill of it. The reality of having to decide on a career path, and dealing with my lover's ex-girlfriend and living in a shared apartment when I have a lover — a girlfriend? — is too, *real*.

I am not ready to make these decisions.

As I step through the apartment door the grim reality of the small space grounds me slightly. I know I cannot continue living here. Regardless. I can't keep working just a bit more than part time and sharing a bed with a roommate. Even if there was no Toni taking my breath away, this reality can't continue.

Chris is in the living room, brows raised at my more-than-likely disheveled appearance. I might even be wearing the same clothes as the last time she saw me, two, no, three days ago.

"Had a good, uh, week, I take it?" she asks amusedly.

I collapse on the couch, more excited, or, maybe, more anxious, than I had realized. "Oh um gee, you'll never guess who stopped by last night."

Chris just looks me.

"Toni is going to break it off with Laurence. So we can explore this thing between us." As I tell Chris this, I realize this is the conversation I want to be thinking about — this conversation centered on *after-Laurence*, not the conversation Toni is likely having with Laurence, right now. I want to understand what this attraction means, where will Toni and I go, where will Toni take me?

As I talk, Chris's expression shifts from entertained to concerned.

At her frown, I blush. "We really connected," I say lamely.

"You know she's basically cheating on her girlfriend... with you," she points out bluntly.

Her reaction isn't what I expect — usually she isn't judgmental. Her mumbo-jumbo beliefs typically have her taking a more liberated approach to things — especially relationships. "It's not really cheating since they're going to split up now," I say defensively.

"But was Laurence on this same page before Toni hooked up with you?" Chris challenges me. "Do you really think this is how healthy relationships usually start?"

Her words sink into my belly. "I know, I know... it just happened..."

Chris reaches over and squeezes my hand supportively. "I get she makes you feel good, but don't get your heart too wrapped up so soon. See how the break up goes first. You don't even know what kind of mess it will end up being. Toni seems captivating," Chris grins ruefully, "and hot, for sure, but getting involved with someone already in a relationship is asking for drama and heartbreak down the road. Are you really willing to risk that?"

There is a seed of doubt in me that her words trigger. Some seed of doubt I think I have been trying to ignore since the first night waking up on the futon with Toni.

"I know you're right, it's just... she makes me feel so alive, you know? Like I'm finally moving into something new and exciting rather than following the same routine every day."

Chris nods understandingly. "I get the appeal. She's pretty, uh, erotic." Chris smiles, "But you don't know her very well. And, honestly, you deserve more than being someone's side piece, Liz. Really, think about yourself here."

"But I am not the side piece now, or won't be, anyway... soon enough." I smile and pop up off the couch. "And, I am gonna be late for work! Gotta change and get out of here." I don't mention that I don't really want to think about this part. The breakup part. The messy part. I don't know Laurence so don't feel badly for her, but, yet, in some way, I do.

Retreating to the bedroom, my mind swirls with conflict. Chris's caution is valid — getting involved with Toni could easily end in heartbreak, and not just for Laurence. What if Laurence has something that she can give Toni that I do not and Toni doesn't make the break? What if this unexpected attraction fades? What am I going to do without university as my excuse for not growing up and getting a job... what if... what if... so many complications.

But I can't resolve anything right now. I pull some clean clothes out of the closet and get dressed for work.

A Bake-Off

I WALK out the employee entrance at the end of my Friday shift. Toni is not here, outside the store, waiting for me. I didn't think I had expected her to be here — I hadn't daydreamed all that much about her while I worked — but the weight of disappointment when I scan the parking area and don't see her car indicates otherwise. Toni is not here. I don't want to think about how her conversation went with Laurence. Or what it means about how that conversation went that Toni is not here to pick me up.

I realize I am still watching for Toni's car when I catch myself looking out the bus window scanning the mall parking lot. I shake my head at myself. I will go home and spend a quiet Friday night figuring out my life. I have to decide if I am going to accept one of the offers for graduate school, and, if I am, which one. Do I want to live as a poor student for another 2 years? Do I want to move cities? Do I want to stay here and... what... ? Does Toni?

Does Toni what?

Why have my thoughts drifted back to Toni again?

This will not be helpful in my decision making. But, as the bus ride home drags on, my mind wanders and I don't seem able to stop it. My imagination fills out the conversation she had with Laurence. I imagine it was dramatic and Laurence didn't take it well. I imagine Toni is waiting for Laurence to calm down, to stop crying, to return to Bathurst — to leave so Toni can come see me.

Toni. Maybe she isn't even interested in more than a fling; maybe Chris is right and I am just setting myself up for heartache. Maybe Toni never intended to break up with Laurence and they are, even now, messing up the sheets that were so freshly changed.

And, maybe that is a good thing. Maybe I need to focus on my own life and not be thinking about a relationship. And, possibly, this is as Toni imagined it would be — us having an open relationship too?

"Whoa, Liz," I chastise myself, hopefully not out loud. Nobody on the bus is looking at me, so probably I wasn't talking out loud to myself. Hah. My first question should be, "Does Toni want a relationship, or, equally important, do I?" and not what the nature of that relationship might be. Toni and I really haven't been out of bed long enough to discuss anything that might lead me to think either of us have thought about a relationship.

As the familiar streets roll by, I try to shove Toni from my thoughts and focus on the life choices before me. Graduate school acceptances sit at home, unacknowledged. And I need to decide whether I want two more years of academics, or if it is time for me to go get a real job.

I need to leave thoughts of Toni out of these decisions.

* * *

Stepping into the small apartment, I see Chris is home again. The lack of privacy, of space to think about my life, magnifies my inability to make decisions. Or, more likely, it will push me into a wrong decision — into a decision I won't have fully thought through.

I must have been standing in the doorway staring at her for several seconds, because Chris looks up from her laptop with a questioning gaze. "Rough day?"

I shake my thoughts away and drop onto the couch. "Not

terrible work-wise, but..." reaching for the solitary ratty throw pillow, I hug it tightly, unsure how to articulate my thoughts.

Chris doesn't wait for me to finish — I am pretty sure she can read my mind. "Toni I assume? You haven't heard from her yet? Or, since?" When I don't even look at her, she closes her laptop and shifts her body to fully face me. "I can listen if you need someone to talk it through with... But you probably already know what I think..."

I do know what she thinks. I know the reasonable answer. But I take a deep breath anyway, "It's just everything all at once, you know? University is done and I still have no idea what I want to do next. Do I apply for jobs? Grad school? Take some time for myself? And then there's Toni..."

My voice trails off as I think of her. Chris prompts gently, "What's going on in your head about Toni?"

"I think I'm afraid to pursue anything with her. Or to trust that she wants to pursue something serious with me." I flush as I realize I have expressed my real concern, my real sticking point. Out loud. What if I am only imagining Toni is real, that she could be real-life for me. "I have huge life changes to decide on. What if I choose wrong. What if it doesn't work out and things get awkward? But I also don't want to miss an opportunity if this could be something real."

I sigh in frustration. "I hate that I have to make these decisions right now, when everything feels so uncertain. I wish I could just freeze time and figure myself out before taking the next step."

Chris nods thoughtfully. "I get why you're feeling overwhelmed. But sometimes you just have to carry on, take a chance, you know? Life doesn't stop while you wait for all the answers to become clear. As for Toni, well — I guess the question you have to answer is whether you think it's worth exploring what you have, even if it ends up being only temporary? Just answering that might bring clarity. And... you probably don't have to decide anything today, or this week, or maybe even this month... maybe just wait for Toni to resolve her relationship with Laurence and stop getting ahead of yourself?"

Her bluntness gives me perspective and eases some of the tightness in my chest. "Yeah, I know, I jump ahead of myself too much. Toni just has me stirred up or something. But I might have been in this head space anyway, with life as I know it ending... Hah."

Chris laughs with me.

"I will think about it over dinner!" I pop up off the couch. "Mac n' cheese? My treat."

"Sounds delish," Chris agrees, "and don't be too hard on yourself if you have thoughts of Toni interfering with your ability to make decisions. Emotions aren't logical. Just focus on you, and give yourself a couple weeks, at least, to see how things shake out. You're fine for now."

Chris returns to her laptop, and I make us some late supper — my specialty: boxed macaroni and cheese, with ground meat. Cheap and yummy. And pretty much the only thing I know how to cook without carefully following a recipe. I pour myself a gin and sip it while I watch the pasta cook. It doesn't take long. I return to the living room with two bowls to find Chris has put her laptop away and has a streamed show on pause on the television.

"Bit of baking show entertainment?" she asks as I hand her a bowl of supper.

"Sure." I sit back on the couch with my own bowl of supper and my new glass of gin, still mulling over our conversation.

Chris presses play and the host tells us it is cake week. The camera pans across the bakers as the host provides the instructions for what the contestants have to do for this challenge.

"Oh, cake. I love cake," Chris says, inanely.

I just nod. The possibilities bopping around in my head — graduate school, a career, moving somewhere new. And then there is Toni... — mean I don't even taste my own dinner, let alone have space to think about how good cake might be, just now.

A while later Chris gets me a refill on her way back from the bathroom. We are now on bread week in the show. I do like bread.

The show, in its mindlessness and safety — there are no warnings for violence or language or smoking or mature themes here — helps me feel better, relaxing my shoulders and blurring the edges of my worries.

As the baking show moves through its season of episodes, I find myself wondering what Toni is up to tonight, how it went with Laurence, where Laurence is now, if Toni is also thinking of me. These thoughts do not bother me. I am calm.

A small smile creeps onto my face as I imagine — remember — Toni spooned behind me, in a seedy motel bed. Maybe Chris is right — maybe I will just hang out with the status quo for now, and see what happens when Toni calls me, see then where this might go.

* * *

At some point I doze off on the couch. The thin band of sunlight that somehow manages to reach our basement apartment window streams in through the open curtains and wakes me. I groan at the dull ache in my neck from falling asleep in an awkward position. I sit up and am surprised to see it is nearly 10 a.m. My drink glass and supper dishes are nowhere in sight, but I don't recall taking them into the kitchen. Chris must have thought I needed the sleep and tidied up without waking me before she went to bed. Though, why she would have left me sleeping on this saggy couch is beyond me.

After a shower and some breakfast, I feel halfway human again. Memories from last night's conversation with Chris float back as I sip my Irish coffee. I wonder when Toni will be calling me. I had hoped it would be this morning — oh, who am I kidding, I had hoped it would have been last night — but as the clock ticks onward, that doesn't look likely.

Eventually I realize it is time to head out, and I make my way to the bus stop to get to work.

My shift at work drags on endlessly. I find it extremely difficult to keep the smile pasted on my face as my coworker chatters incessantly about... something... I don't listen.

My mind is busy, thinking about why I hadn't heard from Toni. Why has she gone silent? Has she changed her mind about Laurence? My overactive imagination conjures up so many scenarios that are, really, all the same. But I can't make myself stop thinking about them.

What if she's with Laurence right now, having decided not to go through with the breakup after all?

It is this not-knowing that is the torture.

As soon as closing time arrives, I take the bus straight home, even though I do, fleetingly, contemplate stopping in at the Pool Queue. Maybe Dawn is there. Maybe Toni. But definitely the Long Islands are.

But I don't stop in. I don't know how I would feel if Toni is there. If she is there with Laurence.

Or if she is there without Laurence. That might actually be worse.

And, besides, I can't afford to be drinking non-happy hour priced Long Islands. Especially when I have a perfectly fine bottle of Gordon's Gin at home.

Chris is not at the apartment when I get there. I fill a large tumbler with ice and grab the Gordon's and head into the bedroom. I strip down to my underwear and pull on a tank top. And I curl up in bed and click the TV on. I look through the favorited shows on Chris's profile — I never really had much time to spend watching TV so never even set up my own profile. I find the baking show we had watched the night before and select Sweet Week. I am pretty sure I didn't see that episode the previous evening.

A couple episodes later, I am just topping up my glass from the bottle on the night stand and I hear a soft knock on the bedroom door. "Liz? Can I come in?" Chris's voice whispers quietly.

"Sure. Only me in here."

She opens the door, "Just wanted to make sure."

"Yeah, I have been a jackass, haven't I... I shouldn't have brought her back here."

She glances at the gin bottle. "You doing okay? I assume you haven't heard from Toni, huh? I got some Sheridan's." She holds the bottle of liqueur out to me, "Shall I grab a couple glasses?"

I take the proffered bottle with a laugh. "You know me too well."

She returns with two heavy bottomed tumblers, both with ice, and settles beside me in the bed. I pour the Sheridan's, and we lean side by side against the headboard and sip them. I am pretty sure this treat won't stop my thoughts from spinning out of control, but I do appreciate the attempt.

Just when I can't stand the silence anymore, she speaks. "Maybe... maybe she just got caught up in something... maybe she had to, I dunno, go home for some family reason," she offers.

I just look at her, and, after a pause, we both laugh out loud. "You need to work on your delivery. More serious... maybe say it like you believe it..." I rub her arm. "But, thanks, I appreciate the attempt."

She just nods.

"Most likely she changed her mind. Or maybe I misread the whole thing. Or Laurence convinced her to stay..."

Chris puts her hand on mine where it rests on her arm. "If that's the case, if any of that's the case, she's not who you need in your life, and you probably dodged a very messy situation, at the least."

The chat, and the liqueur treat, and maybe the gin, are calming. I take a deep breath, "yeah, I will stop working through these scenarios in my head and just carry on with my life. Toni wasn't in it at all a few weeks ago, no need to dwell on her not being in it now. I need to stop this foolishness. I am a grown ass woman. And...look — it's the bake-off finale... wonder who will win."

A Secret Encore

TIME PASSES

I **WORK** as many shifts as my employer makes available, so, pretty much full time. Which is great for two reasons: it keeps me occupied so I don't dwell on my lack of, well, money and love and time and goals, and I need to start gathering money. I have accepted a graduate position at a university in Toronto. I am aiming to get there in late August, and to save as much money as I can between now and then. My employer has agreed to transfer me to a part-time position in a store up there. And I will get a small assistantship from the university. It will, no doubt, be pretty tight money-wise, but that's the price of being a student.

I am not totally convinced I am okay with another two years of student-level poverty, but the move to Toronto will bring me to a new head space, a new place. And the two years will fly by, I am sure.

And then... I am walking back through the mall to return to work after spending my meal break sipping coffee in the food court when I see her walking toward me as I walk toward the store where I work. She slows as she draws close. Our eyes meet. I hesitate, unsure if I even want to stop, if I want to have this conversation — any conversation — with her, or if I can just keep walking, past her, and leave her behind.

But Toni holds out one arm, palm up, her eyes asking me to stop. I want to... I plan to... keep walking. My feet, however, seem to have a different plan and I stop.

Toni closes the distance between us. "Hey, I'm glad I caught up to you. Can we talk?" Her tone is soft, her lips full, her eyes dark and dreamy and...

I sigh, "I don't know if that's a good idea, Toni." I don't elaborate and tell her I think it will be a waste of both our time.

"Please, I just want to explain." She gazes at me with those intense brown eyes, and I find myself unable to refuse. I move toward the bench outside my store's doors and we sit. She sits sideways, her left leg tucked up under her right, facing me.

For a moment, neither of us speak. I can feel Toni studying my face, as if trying to read my thoughts. "So..." she begins, "I know... it... ah... things have been confusing. I know I should have come by to see you..."

I let out a dry laugh. "That's an understatement."

Toni reaches over slowly, as if asking permission, and takes my hand in hers. Her touch sends a jolt through me, even as my mind orders me to pull away, to walk away. "I never meant to lead you on. Being with you that week...it made me realize some things."

My pulse quickens at the memory of *that week*, but I try to stay in this present moment, not back in the moments that belonged to that week. "Realize what, exactly?"

She sighs. "You know my relationship with Laurence wasn't working. I care about her, but not in the way she wants and not the way I care about you." Toni's eyes flick back and forth on mine as she maintains eye contact. "I really planned to break things off with her. But, that weekend, when she came, she had gotten an apartment already, and quit her job and she wants to start a life here. With me. I couldn't tell her about you. I didn't have the heart to tell her."

"So you didn't even tell her about us?" My heart sinks.

"I did, I did! Just, not right away. Not when she got here and we moved from the motel to our — her — new apartment on the Monday."

"That was two weeks ago Toni."

"I can't stop thinking about you. I want to give us a real chance, Liz, if you'll let me try again."

Her words catch me off guard, dragging up hopes I'd tried to push down. This spark of hope nearly overwhelms me, but, just as suddenly, reality pulls me back. "What took you so long to end it then? I wait and not a peep. Nothing. I didn't hear from you at all, until now?"

Toni lowers her head. "I know, I'm sorry. It wasn't easy. Laurence is really hurt and upset. I needed time to sort through my feelings and be sure this was the right choice."

She finally meets my gaze again, and I see — or maybe I want to see — sincerity. My walls of determination start to crumble. Toni gives my hand a gentle squeeze. "I understand if you need more space or don't fully trust me. But my feelings for you are real. I'm willing to prove that however I can, if you'll give me a chance."

Her words stir up so many emotions — hope, uncertainty, longing. Her attraction is magnetic. I can feel, even now, the pull. This attraction is almost unbearable. I catch myself looking at her lips. "So, where is Laurence now? Where are you staying?"

Toni doesn't even blush when she answers, "I am still staying at the apartment. But just for now."

"With Laurence? How... is she okay with that?" I know I would not be. There is not even a chance I would consider living in this type of situation — as the victim anyway.

Toni would have been out on her ass as soon as she confessed, if it were me. I don't tell her this though.

And, with Toni still staying there, can I trust her? Can I trust Laurence? How will I know that they won't spark up old feelings, or how can I know that Toni isn't just chasing thrills with me and this won't just end up hurting me again, in another two weeks' time when Toni decides the excitement is not as exciting if

Laurence isn't in the wings, creating the rush behind the threat of discovery, of tears and screaming and crying.

As if sensing my inner conflict, Toni speaks softly, "Take all the time you need. I'm not going anywhere. When you're ready to talk again, you know my phone number." She releases my hand in what feels like slow motion and stands.

I don't ask the main — the only — question I have on my mind because I realize I don't want to hear the answer: "Are you still sleeping with her?" I want to ask. I really want to.

But I also don't.

The *don't* wins out. I don't want this answer, and that should tell me more than I am willing to admit.

Our eyes meet one last time before she turns to leave. I watch her go, wrestling with everything she'd said. My thoughts are so tangled, I can't sift through the mess. I want to follow her and take her back to bed. I want her to take me back to her bed. But. That bed has had — has? — another woman in it.

I need a drink.

* * *

When I get home, Chris takes one look at my face and knows something is up. I recount the whole conversation as we sit on the couch together. I sip my drink, she sips her coffee, and she listens without judgment. Or, almost without judgment.

"Liz. You know this answer. It seems Toni likes her cake — a lot," Chris says. "She can't keep living with her ex and expect you to date her. And, do you even know what the ex — Laurence — knows? Did Toni actually break up with her? I can't believe Laurence would allow Toni to stay living there if they did break up." Chris's words echo my own thoughts nearly exactly.

Chris continues, "Yeah. You know the answer Liz. You need to put her out of your mind, there's no way you can trust her, let alone work on a relationship with her."

I sigh. "That's just it — I don't know if I can put her out of my mind. I don't know if I want to. I haven't stopped thinking about her in the two weeks she was gone, so how am I supposed to just stop thinking about her now? I think she is just, confused, struggling with hurting Laurence, and that's it. Just letting her leave today, without saying anything, without saying yes, was nearly impossible. All I wanted to do was..."

"Take her to bed..." Chris finishes my sentence for me. "Liz. It's just physical. You've never had a girlfriend, a serious one anyway, so you don't even have a base to gauge from."

I tense. Chris sees this and shrugs. "Okay, okay... let's not think in absolutes right now. Take some more time, you don't have to decide everything right now; if she's there at all, she'll be there tomorrow or next week, or whenever you're ready... see how you feel. You don't owe Toni anything. Focus on you and what's best for your well-being."

Her words, and a refill on both our drinks, help bring me some calm.

But thoughts of Toni's smile, her touch, her mouth, on my mouth, on me, keep creeping into my thoughts.

I pour another glass of whiskey, already feeling the buzz from my first two. Glancing at the clock, I see it's already after 10. I know I should stop. I work in the morning. I toss back the drink and head into the kitchen to pour another.

And there is a knock at the apartment door.

Chris answers it.

I return to the living room and, when I see Toni, a weird bubbly weight drops into my stomach. I am tempted to just turn around and lock myself in the bedroom.

Chris walks toward me and waves at Toni, in the doorway. "You need closure on this. Go talk to her. You deserve answers, and some peace of mind either way."

I know she is right.

Toni looks hopeful and yet uncertain. "Hey. I wasn't sure if you'd talk to me. But I couldn't not stop by."

I meet her gaze steadily. "I needed more time to think."

Toni smiles softly. "Of course." She looks into my eyes, just like they do on TV — gazing seriously. "You said, *needed*, are you done thinking now?"

Taking a steadying breath, I break eye contact with her. "Toni... pursuing anything further wouldn't be smart or fair to anyone involved. As much as I enjoyed our week together, a casual fling isn't what I'm looking for right now." My words come out more firmly than I had expected. "I am going to Toronto, for university. In the fall," I add.

And Toni smiles. "How 'bout we go for a drink. It can be in celebration of your move. And maybe we can talk." She looks over my shoulder where I imagine Chris is standing, listening to us.

The pull to Toni is strong and, against my better judgment, and clearly against Chris's as well, as I hear her huff behind me, I nod, my heart flipping in my chest at the thought of watching Toni's mouth as we talk.

Chris does speak up, "Liz, you said you needed space from her. Another drink isn't space."

I know her concern is genuine but I brush it off, somehow oddly eager to slip back under Toni's spell. "Meh, it's fine Chris. And, besides, I am going to Toronto. That will be tons of space." I look into Toni's eyes, "This will just be for fun."

Toni pulls me close for a half hug, half grope that sends butter-flies through my stomach. "I am so glad you can't resist me," she whispers in my ear before she tries to capture my lips in a kiss. I don't give in to her temptation, though I feel the jolt it sends down into my abdomen.

* * *

The pub, not surprisingly, is crowded. There is nobody sitting at the bar so we pull two of the bar stools away from the others and set them close together at the end farthest from where the bartender usually stands. Toni orders two rum and colas and we sip them and gaze into each other's eyes.

48

The current that pulls me to her is electric. We slide our bar stools very close together and our hands find each other under the cover of the bar top. We don't talk much. I don't think either of us know what to say. Or maybe neither of us wants to say what it is that needs to be said.

By the time our third drink arrives, Toni's fingertips glide up and down my thigh, higher on each stroke. My fingertips reciprocate. And then our fingertips are stroking, rubbing, each other through our jeans.

"Come back with me." Her voice is husky and her hand is insistent.

Knowing what will come next, I swallow the end of my drink. She doesn't break eye contact as she swallows the end of hers.

* * *

This time a cab takes us to what must be the apartment Laurence had rented. When Toni kisses me full mouthed while she fumbles with the building entrance key, I pull my mouth away long enough to ask, "What about Laurence?"

She finally gets the door unlocked and her mouth consumes mine again, greedily. Then we separate long enough to make it up two flights of stairs, to an apartment door. "She's gone..." my heart leaps in that moment before Toni continues, "home for the weekend."

And then we're in the apartment and Toni is leading me down a hallway to a bedroom with an open door and she pulls me gently into the room and grabs my shirt at my waist and pulls it up over my head before pushing me gently back onto the bed.

And I pull her shirt up over her head and reach behind her and unhook her bra and after a minute or two of her nipples taking turns in my mouth, the rest of our clothing is hurriedly discarded and the bedspread is pushed off onto the floor so we are naked on the top sheet, and our hands and lips and mouth explore each other's wetness with a burning urgency.

At the back of my mind, I am aware that there is there is a thrill here, unrelated to Toni's mouth on me. This risky behavior, in Laurence's bed, in Laurence's apartment, under an assumption that Laurence probably — probably — won't walk in on us, heightens every sensation. And I cry out loudly when I come.

* * *

After, lying sleepily in Toni's arms, I pointedly ignore the doubts creeping in. This was what I wanted, it has to be, or I wouldn't have come here. I know what this is: just a fun goodbye, a version of 'one for the road'. I tell myself that making the decision to go to Toronto wouldn't have been so easy if it wasn't the right one. If I had wanted this more, wanted Toni more, for real, I would not have decided on graduate school in Toronto. This, here, now, is only a final closure on this loop.

But. Lying here against her, feeling her warmth and smelling her scent, makes walking away now, moving to Toronto now, seem impossible. And, with her fingers tracing patterns on my bare skin so tenderly and the taste of her on my lips, I start to mention this to her. To ask what we do next, now.

Before I can speak, though, Toni rolls over toward me, on top of me, tugging the top sheet with her so we are covered. She covers my mouth with hers and slides a thigh between mine, and shifts so her wetness is pressing down on my thigh, and slowly rocks against me, against herself, and back, with increasing speed and urgency and pressure until she suddenly presses her face into my hair and grunts. She relaxes and rolls partly off me. My wet thigh gets cool, even under the top sheet folded over us, and we fall asleep, her curled against me.

* * *

We wake up well past noon. I miss my Saturday shift at work in its entirety, and the rest of the day — the rest of the weekend —

50

passes in a blur of bedsheets and Irish coffees and couch top and, once, kitchen chair while empty pizza boxes toppled over onto the floor beside us. It's not until Sunday very late afternoon that Toni suggests it's time I slip out.

"I don't know when Laurence might be back. But, you know, we don't want you to cross paths."

I don't say anything. There isn't anything to say. So I help Toni strip the sheets from the bed and watch as she stuffs them in the washer.

She embraces me at the door and we kiss, a very long, very invasive kiss and I am just getting ready to slip my hands back down her pants when she pulls away, breathless. "You have to go... I can't... I will come see you tomorrow."

And, with that, I let myself out of Laurence's apartment building and into a beautiful Sunday early evening. I haven't been outside since our walk from my place to the Pool Queue on Friday night. And I haven't had clothes on since early Saturday morning. They feel odd, and constricting, and dirty, from laying two days in a pile on the floor at the end of Laurence's bed.

I walk home, enjoying the pleasant May weather. Chris is not there when I arrive, so I shower and head to bed. I have not had a lot of sleep in the past two days and am exhausted. And sore, I smile to myself as I fall asleep. The overnight break will be nice.

* * *

The next evening Toni does come to see me. But she does not come in. In the face of Chris's obvious, and voiced, disapproval of what she calls my poor choices in women, Toni and I decide to go for a long drive, which ends up being a short one to a secluded place at the edge of a local treed park.

The week passes in a blur of secret trysts. I go to work, Toni picks me up outside the employee entrance and we drive to the back of a parking lot, or the edge of the park, or, once, to the back of the dark parking lot outside the Pool Queue.

Chris's disapproval does not lessen. "You're going to get hurt," she says one night as I stumble in past midnight. "And what kind of story is Toni making up to explain these... uh... *dates* you two are having?"

I know she is right. I know this cannot go on. I can't keep meeting Toni in secret and slipping into the backseat of her car under the overhang of trees at the back of the parking lot of the local park, waiting for the night that Laurence will be away visiting someone so that Toni and I can swap the backseat of Toni's car for the sheet top of Laurence's bed. But I am too far under Toni's spell to care — about consequences, about Laurence, about my future in Toronto, which I have not yet discussed with Toni, other than that one time, before spending the weekend naked with her and second-guessing the whole moving-to-Toronto plan.

* * *

Then, on Friday, I am at the liquor store near my apartment when I see Toni with a petite dark-haired woman at the checkout, with two bottles of red wine in front of them. Toni's hand rests in the small of the woman's back and I realize suddenly this must be Laurence. She pays with a card and leans into Toni, looking up at her and smiling. Toni's lips move but I am too far away, and frozen in place, so can't hear what she says.

With what feels like knives twisting in my gut, I force myself to continue walking toward the checkout as they start to walk away from it, toward the exit doors. I almost stop, and duck behind a shelf of wine, and wait for them to clear the space, so they don't see me, but I refuse to let myself.

As I approach, Toni looks in my direction and sees me.

I wait for her to look back at Laurence and ignore me. To tighten her arm around Laurence's waist and escort her the rest of the way out the door before Laurence can see me — before Toni is forced to acknowledge me here, under the bright lights of the liquor store.

But Toni doesn't move away, and she says something quietly to Laurence, who then turns to look at me. I set the bottle of gin down on the counter and the guy behind it scans it and tells me my total and I tap my card and pick up my bottle and step toward them, still standing there, facing me, at the end of the checkout area, just inside the exit doors, as if they are waiting for me.

"Laurence, voici Liz," Toni introduces me as I get close.

Laurence looks at me with her pretty blue eyes and long lashes and delicate features. "Enchantée, j'ai beaucoup entendu parler de toi."

I am speechless. I don't know what to say. I don't know what she has heard about me. What Toni has told her. What she means. And I guess, clearly, I hadn't actually believed Toni had mentioned me to Laurence.

Toni laughs, breaking the awkward silence. "Oh, les femmes. Ça va, ne vous inquiétez pas..." and she steps toward me, "Liz, it's fine."

Laurence's eyes do not tell me the same story.

Toni embraces me briefly, she starts to say something, but I pull away before she can. "Je dois filer. Enchantée, Laurence. Toni." I nod and walk briskly out the exit door.

* * *

I walk the short walk home with a heavy dread settling in my stomach, the magnitude of the situation fully dawning on me. The shame is heavy. Laurence. Toni. My life on hold for a series of quickies in the backseat of a car. I pour myself a generous drink. And another. And, eventually, I find myself waking up in the bed I share with Chris, my pillow wet and Chris rubbing my back while she murmurs some words of consolation I can't hear through the humiliation that flushes hot in my face.

One Future

THE POOL QUEUE is bustling for a Thursday night as I weave through the crowd in search of an open table. A baseball game plays silently on one of the many televisions scattered around. Scanning the room, I finally spot a small high-top table in the back corner that is miraculously unoccupied.

I am just about to drape my jacket over the back of one of the three stools at the table and am gauging the line up at the bar when a familiar flash of excitement thrills up through my belly at the sight of Toni sitting alone at the end of the bar counter, nursing a drink with an uncharacteristically downcast expression.

It hasn't even been a week since I saw her and Laurence at the liquor store, so I guess I shouldn't be surprised at the spark of desire, and fear, that spins through me.

My feelings are so conflicting I don't know if I should leave quietly before she sees me, or if I should just give in and join her, again, knowing where that will take us. I want to not care where it takes us. But I think I do. But I don't know how to suppress this attraction, this compulsion to be with her. To feel her naked and wet and female...

Chemistry, or biology, or insanity, resolves my dilemma and

before I know it, my feet are carrying me toward where she is sitting at the bar, even as my nerves twist my stomach into knots.

Toni must have sensed my approach. Her gaze flicks up through her long lashes and I imagine I see a spark of cautious hope. Up close, I see signs of exhaustion pulling at her features and her normally expressive eyes seem dimmed, the smile she offers me not quite reaching them.

"Fancy seeing you here," I venture, settling onto the empty stool beside her.

She looks at me and does not break eye contact. "It's not accidental."

"I figured. Everything okay?" I don't know why I ask. I can tell everything is not okay. It's not okay for her, and it's not okay for me. I didn't even know it wasn't okay for me, until right now, here, looking at her.

She manages a hollow laugh. "About as okay as it can be, I guess. Breakups are always an crazy mess, even when you know they're for the best." Her fingers toy with the condensation on her glass. She looks down at her fingers playing with her glass. "Liz. I miss you."

My instinct is to respond. To tell her I have this ache deep in my belly, from missing her. But I resist, maintaining a guarded distance for both our sakes. "I can relate."

Toni nods, taking a slow sip from her drink. "I really needed to see you. Chris wouldn't tell me your schedule. I don't know how to see you at work. You are never home, or never answer the phone anyway. I thought I would try here. Again. Tonight."

A fluff of thrill fills me at her words, but I can tell by her voice, her quietness, that she has had more than the one drink she is nursing now. "You've been here awhile, waiting?"

"Pretty sure this is my third – or fourth? drink. I had no idea when you might come, if you might..." She waves distractedly at her glass, eyebrows furrowing as if trying to solve a complicated equation.

Despite myself, concern creeps in, "Maybe you should call it a night after this one, then. Don't want you doing something you'll regret later."

Her eyes catch mine with an unexpected clarity that sends a shiver through me, her face so open the look on it steals my breath. "I am not doing anything else that I will regret. I am done doing regret. I – never mind. You're probably right."

An awkward pause falls as I wait for Toni to elaborate on what she'd almost revealed. But a wall seems to have dropped into place around her. The bartender chooses that moment to arrive, expression questioning if I wanted something. My throat has gone dry.

"Long Island, please." At least the alcohol will give me something to focus on other than Toni's magnetism which has me teetering on the edge of control, on the edge of sensible decisions.

"I miss you. And am not dealing with it well, clearly," she admits with a wave at her drink. "Pathetic, I know."

I know I shouldn't even entertain rekindling anything with her.

But I also know it's not a re-anything. The kindle never went anywhere. It's here, burning in my groin, and my belly, and making my face flush.

She graces me with the ghost of a real smile, small but full of... something. "Have I mentioned lately that I miss you?"

"Once or twice when drunk, maybe," I tease gently.

A chuckle escapes her. "Yeah. I love you Liz."

My stomach literally flops over and I hear a rushing in my ears. Did she just say that? And then I hear myself speak, as if I am far away, "I love you too Toni." But then I think I do manage to check my tongue just before the words slip out.

But not before the truth of them settles heavy in my chest.

Her look holds my eyes. Warm tremors run down my spine, and I am certain I can see a flicker of hope reigniting in the dark chocolate eyes holding mine far too intimately. And yet, not nearly intimately enough. No, not intimately enough.

Clearing my throat, I scan the bar to break eye contact, desperate to steer us away from this, from here, from what might exist. I am moving to Toronto. This can never work. The bartender places my drink in front of me and, grateful, I take a long sip.

We drink in silence. For some time. I don't know what to say. And she has already said everything she can.

"How about some fresh air – get us away from more alcohol temptation, too. Nothing like a nice breezy walk to clear the head."

Toni studies me a moment and eventually nods, dropping a bill onto the counter and sliding mostly smoothly off her stool.

* * *

And then we are walking the familiar route toward my apartment. There is no pressure to fill the silence.

Finally her soft voice breaks the quiet, "You know, I've been thinking." I pause our walk to wait for her to go on.

Toni focuses determinedly ahead as if gathering courage, shoving her hands in her pockets as if against a sudden chill, or maybe a sudden urge to do something else with them. "This past week made me realize how I've felt for a while. And that I am clinging to routine and familiarity out of comfort. I don't want to be with Laurence, I want to be with you..."

I interrupt her, "I'm moving to Toronto..."

She interrupts me back, "I know, you told me. For graduate school."

I am mildly surprised this fact had stuck with her, that she had believed me, that she remembered, that she had paid attention to that detail when, at the time, I was more focused on her nakedness, and her mouth on me, than on whether or not I was truly going move to Toronto.

I don't speak, but we start walking again. Our strides match, and she puts her arm around me.

"What I'm trying to say is... I think I need a fresh start some-where new to really move on with my life. Find out who I am, who you and I can be together, without all those lingering expectations and this history weighing me down, you know?" Toni takes in a

57

deep breath. "Yeah." She stares fixedly ahead as if solving a puzzle. "You told me you were starting grad school in Toronto in the fall. I was thinking maybe... it could give me a chance at a fresh start, too, give us both a fresh start, if..."

The unspoken question hangs heavy in the charged space between us, my pulse suddenly deafening in my own ears. "If what?" I prompt as carefully as my hammering heart will allow.

Toni stops again, turning to face me fully with an open vulnerability I'd never seen before. Her hands find mine, hot palms sending electric tingles up my arms. "If I went with you. To Toronto, I mean. We could... I don't know, give this thing between us a real shot without all the messy history. If you were open to the idea, that is."

Blinking rapidly, I struggle to process the implications. I can have Toni, without the specter of Laurence always there, always making me wonder if, or when, Toni will be sucked back into that life with Laurence, and I can still go to graduate school and move forward on figuring out what my future might look like. I can work toward a future that doesn't have me sharing a bed with a roommate in order to make ends meet. Everything that might be — with Toni, with love, with a future that didn't require my family's buy-in — hangs waiting in the fragile space between my racing heartbeats.

And I hear myself answer before I am even aware of what I am going to say. "A fresh start. That's what I was going to be doing with my move to Toronto, on my own... I think... I think if you want to give this... what's between us... a real shot, I think a fresh start would do us both good, Toni. And this way we will never have to wonder 'what if.'"

Her answering smile holds all the thrill I recall from our first meeting. Toni steps closer, arms slipping around my waist as mine entwine behind her neck.

"I'd like that. A lot." Her breath ghosts against my lips, she is close enough that, even under street lamp light, I can see the flecks of very dark brown dancing within the dark brown eyes that swallow me up.

Toni's arms feel steady and sure around me, filling me with a sense of comfort and safety I haven't felt since before the weekend Toni moved in with Laurence instead of dumping her for me. The attraction still burns just below my belly, too. I gaze into her eyes, just now allowing myself to realize she has said she loves me, and she wants to move to Toronto with me, to be with me, to make an *us*, into the future.

"I'm glad," I mumble, "— very glad. But are you absolutely sure about this? I don't want you to have any regrets."

She nods, "I've never been more sure of anything. Being with you makes me realize how it's supposed to feel. I think in Toronto, I won't have all the baggage holding me back, holding us back."

Her words wash over me, easing so many worries I hadn't consciously realized I had. She leans in, her kiss soft and full of promise. Her mouth firm and insistent, and tender at the same time. My heart pumps loud in my ears.

As we make our way to my apartment hand in hand, I feel a lightness in my step I haven't felt in a long time.

Part 2: Toronto

TRAVEL COSTS

THE SWELTERING JULY heat hits me like a wall as I exit the subway. I trudge the last few blocks home to the apartment.

As I head down the stairs into our apartment, the air gets much cooler, even without air conditioning. This is the — much appreciated — side effect of living in a basement apartment. There may not be much in terms of a view, or even daylight, for that matter, but it is much, much cooler down here in the dark dingy basement. Okay, so it's not really dingy. It just feels dingy because it's small and dark and, while cheap for Toronto standards, is too pricey for a single income.

As I exit the bottom of the stairwell and step into the living room, the temperature drops even lower and becomes almost comfortable. Toni is sprawled on her back on the couch with the classified section of a newspaper folded in half resting on her chest, bare legs dangling over the armrest. She is still wearing the tee she slept in. But, as she turns her head to watch me walk toward her, she takes my breath away.

A little throb of irritation over this pulses in my throat for a second. I swallow it down.

"No luck?" I ask half-heartedly. I drop my bag and collapse

into the small space at the end of the couch, next to her head. "How's it been going?"

Toni shrugs. "Nothing that catches my interest. There must be something better than barista or temp admin positions."

"Toni, we're barely scraping by on my pay alone. I know you might not find something interesting or glamorous, but you need to find something — literally any job — to help out financially. Once we get some regular income coming in, that's when you can look for something better."

She sits up and meets my eyes, a sad expression on her face. It doesn't help me feel any better, but I soften my tone anyway, taking her hands. "I'm just stressed. I want us to feel secure here, together. When the university semester starts I won't be able to work these hours..."

Toni nods slowly, drawing me close. Her familiar scent comforts me and I try very hard to relax into her arms, to somehow move back from the stress and tension that twangs between us. Well, from me. I don't know that there is much stress and tension in her at all. I wonder if I envy this.

"I know. Moving was a big adjustment — I'm still finding my footing. I have another batch of applications submitted though, something should work out, soon."

Kissing her cheek, I force a smile.

She turns her head and captures my lips with hers. She moves to push me back into the couch but I resist. "Sorry Toni, I need to eat. And shower. It's been a long day."

She smiles. "Okay, how 'bout you jump in the shower and I'll whip up something for dinner. Then we can curl up in front of the computer and do some job searching..." Her optimism sounds forced.

When I return to the living room, she has noodles with vegetables ready to serve. We eat in mostly silence. I am tired after a long shift, and a long commute, and she hasn't done anything worth talking about, other than surfing the internet, theoretically in search of work, but, some tiny thread of doubt makes me wonder.

Toronto's job market is pretty robust and it's been weeks without her having any "luck".

"Thanks for dinner, it was great," I say as I settle onto the couch. Toni plops down beside me with her laptop and pulls me into her side, cuddling me against her. She opens the laptop and closes her social media. She double clicks a browser on the task bar and it opens immediately to a job site.

"No problem. The store across the street had fresh veg on clearance." She starts skimming through the job site postings, which are unfiltered and sorted by date posted.

The first posting is for a barista. "I'd get bored dealing with coffee orders all day," she comments.

I hold back a sigh. The next is for an administrative assistant. "No way, being a glorified secretary sounds terrible."

My frustration starts to rise but I bite my tongue. The third is a receptionist at a gym. "And smile cheerfully all day while sweaty people ask me for extra towels? I'll pass."

"Toni, you're being way too picky. We need the money." I say, trying to keep my voice even. "You can apply for any of those..."

She ignores me, dismissing the next few with more critiques. "Physically demanding warehouse work is out. Door to door sales? They still do that? Must be a scam, nobody would open the door to a salesperson anymore..."

I feel a headache coming on. Another listing catches her eye. "Ugh, cold calling people all day to make sales? No thanks."

"I'm busting my ass to support us. You need to be more flexible here," I say sharply. I think I can taste my own frustration in my throat.

Toni huffs. "And settle for something that makes me miserable? How is that going to work?"

Maybe apply a search filter then, for jobs that are okay for you to consider, I think, but don't say. I rub my temples, "I'm too tired for this." I head to the bedroom. "I'm going to bed. I just need to get some sleep."

She watches me go. "It's only 8 p.m., Liz. That's ridiculous."

When I don't stop, she continues, "I've been home alone all day Liz. What am I supposed to do all evening now?"

I don't answer her. I don't have anything nice to say.

I know it's too early to go to bed. I know I shouldn't be as tired as I am. I know I should go back out there and we should cuddle and kiss and fool around and then make our way to the bedroom together.

But I can't.

I want to crawl into the bed and pull the sheet over my head and not come out again.

I don't recall waking up when Toni crawls into bed beside me.

* * *

Morning comes too soon, tugging me from my dreamless sleep. Toni is facing away from me. I didn't wake when she came to bed. I head to the tiny kitchen space and start the coffee brewing — Toni had prepared it last night and I just have to hit the power button. I stand there staring blankly at the coffee machine while I wait for it to finish. Toni emerges sleep-rumpled, and joins me in watching the coffee maker. She stands behind me with her arms around me and hugs me. The machine eventually gargles itself to as close to finished as I will wait for and I pour two mugs of it. We take our coffees to the couch.

Toni pops open her laptop. I sip my coffee and plan out my day. Or, more accurately, plan out my transportation to and from the day. I want to make it to campus to meet my research assistantship supervisor, and my thesis advisor, and, from what I understand, some classmate who will be working with me in order to complete her own thesis, and then to work and home again before it's bedtime, again.

When we moved here, I was not prepared for the time investment involved in commuting. I miss my undergrad years, where the longest commute was 20 minutes. I had tried to find an apartment close to university, or even to one of my jobs, but wasn't able to find an affordable place near one or the other of my destinations.

Work had transferred me to a store in the middle of nowhere, well, north of North York anyway, and by the time I realized it was so far from my cheap housing location that I would have been better off finding a new job rather than being transferred, I was already at my new job. I didn't have the time or energy to find a job closer to home, assuming there was even such a thing that would accommodate my upcoming university schedule.

"I got an interview! Today. Pretty short notice, good thing I am not at work already, huh?" Toni shouts excitedly next to me on the couch, startling me out of my thoughts.

I lean into her and put my free arm around her and snuggle. "That's terrific." I can almost literally feel stress lifting off my shoulders.

Toni quickly finishes the rest of her coffee. We share a long good-morning kiss, then she heads off for a shower.

* * *

When I finally make it home from my long day, I know from her excitement that she has finally found a job.

A couple blissful weeks pass in our new routines. The temperatures don't decrease outside, but our apartment stays mainly cool, and Toni is working and money is not quite as tight, though I think we will need a couple more months of me working two jobs to catch up on the cost of moving and the delay in Toni's job start, but hope is on the horizon, and I think that by the end of the fall semester, I should be able to drop back to just a part-time job and focus fully on my studies.

Then one Thursday evening, as I descend the stairs into the apartment I swear I can feel the tension in the air. Toni is pacing the small living space.

I drop my bag to the floor. "Toni? What happened?"

She abruptly stops pacing and holds my gaze with her deep dark eyes. "I quit my job today."

All breath leaves me at once. "What? Why?"

Toni steps toward me and tries to take my hands. I pull them away and pin them to my sides. A rushing panic sends tingles up my neck. "It just wasn't feeling right. The work is so mind-numbingly dull. I would have lost my mind if I stayed there. And they kept giving me shit for being late..."

Heat rises within my chest. Into my face. "So you just quit? You didn't think to discuss it first? I don't suppose you have another job lined up?"

"I needed an out, Liz! Being trapped in such a soul-sucking job with the other guy looking over my shoulder all the time and counting how many minutes I spend in the toilet... was just too much." Toni's voice rises nearly to a shout, her fists clenching tensely at her sides.

The rush into my face reverses its route and I feel faint from the deflation. As I realize any hopes I had of leaving my overnight job just evaporated, I fight to stay grounded. "I understand feeling trapped, believe me. But we're barely getting by as it is..."

She scoffs, "So I'm just supposed to rot away mindlessly for a paycheck? That's no way to live."

What about me. I want to scream.

But instead I struggle to keep my emotions under control. "No, but you could have looked at finding another job before quitting this one..."

Toni just sighs. "I have to consider my own well-being... I just couldn't do that job. I can't wake up each day wondering how long I will have to stand there listening to those idiots complain about everything I do. I couldn't bring myself to go back, at all."

I swallow the urge to cry. "Toni. I don't want to wake up in that state either, but I do. I can't work full time and go to school and we can't live off my income alone. We can't... I don't know what else to do."

Nearly as quickly as it arose, my anger drains and only a deep weariness remains. A weariness so deep I can't even speak. I can't express my disappointment, my panic.

Toni hugs me. "I know. I'm sorry. We're both exhausted and stressed. Let's get some rest. We can talk about it tomorrow, and figure out a plan, okay?"

We get ready for bed in a tense silence. Sleep, however, does not elude me in my state of exhaustion, and I sleep soundly until dawn.

A Project

THE AIR HUMS with other conversations from the tables around me as I wait in the dimly lit bar, the flickering lights from the dance floor casting a flashing sparkly glow over me, and over the bartender who has been busily pouring drinks for the constant stream of early arrivers, all of us taking advantage of happy hour pricing. The scent of stale beer and the heavy thump of the bass mix the DJ is warming up with fill the air.

Cherry pats me on the shoulder and slides onto a stool next to me. "Been here long?"

"Nope. First drink," I lie, as I finish off my third and push it to the back of the counter. Cherry has good timing, the bartender is in a lull and comes right over.

"I'll have another. Cherry, what are you having?"

"Just soda water. We're working," she smiles.

"Really?" I don't know Cherry at all. We met just before the start of the semester when our shared thesis advisor determined our projects would be so well aligned that we should work together on them. Maybe she never drinks.

But, then again, if she's okay to meet in a bar — to participate in a research project which has bars as one of the key research areas — she must be okay being around alcohol.

"No silly, we aren't sitting in a nightclub with all these hot women," she waves her arm to indicate the other women around us, "and remaining sober. I don't get out much, you know."

"Well, that is a relief. I don't know that it would be much fun to hang out here fully sober."

We are doing research for our projects for our university program. My project is on the role of bar culture in lesbian community and her project, which is way more confusing to me, is on observing a researcher while they make their observations. She will be observing me as I do my research, to determine how her presence influences my research, and, possibly, how my presence influences how I research, or who... or, anyway, something like that. My brain is too full of all the other things I have to do — for university, for work, in my home life — for it to try to understand things that are, effectively, someone else's job.

And I am tired, no, I am beyond tired — I am well into the realm of exhaustion, and it's only week three of university. I know it's the working schedule — the paid job part — which is causing the exhaustion, but I can't see how I can drop any of my paying jobs; I work 10 hours a week on campus, doing research, 20 hours a week working at a store in a mall, and 24 hours a week doing night shift security. All on top of my graduate program, which is, all by itself, supposed to be a full-time job. And it is apparent I won't be able to rely on Toni to help with any of this. Yet anyway.

I stop thinking and focus on my drink.

Cherry ends up getting the same drink as I do, a Long Island Iced Tea, and takes a long drink of it. "Shall we find a table in a corner that is a little more... discreet... we have some serious people watching to do."

We walk across the seating area between the bar and the dance floor and find an empty table along the back wall. We sit side by side, facing outward toward the dance floor.

She starts to explain her project and I let the words flow over my head for several minutes before I interrupt her, "Sorry Cherry. I don't think this is going to work just now. Tonight. I'm not even sure what language you're speaking, let alone what you hope to get out of this watching the watcher thing..."

The alcohol has made me direct, but Cherry isn't fazed. "You just ignore me. Do whatever you would be doing as part of your research and pretend I am not here. And, right now, you can practice pretending I am not here while I swing by the little girl's room, then the bar. Want anything?"

Nodding my head at the offer of a drink, I look at her closely. Her Italian-Canadian heritage is evident in the rich olive tone of her skin and her expressive eyes. They are a deep shade of hazel, closer to brown than green, and I am certain they reflect what is more than likely a fiery temperament. Her dark hair rests on her shoulders and frames her face in a way that accentuates her features.

She sticks her tongue out at me, "Stop staring. I might get the wrong idea." Her lips are full — inviting — and my eyes won't look away from them. I wonder how she kisses, then suddenly clip that thought short and look away from her, over toward the bar.

"Sure, yeah, I'll have another Long Island." I know my thoughts, and this sudden unexpected attraction, are completely attributable to the alcohol.

I watch her as she walks toward the washrooms. I watch other people watch her walk to the washrooms. She moves smoothly, with confidence, like it is perfectly reasonable for a straight woman to come to a lesbian bar to watch a lesbian watch lesbians.

It may be the case that my project ends up being about how the watched watch the watchers.

Cherry eventually returns with drinks for both of us.

I get our next round.

Then, time just slips away. I keep half an eye out for Toni. She knew I was coming here with a classmate to do some work on our research projects. I expected to see her show up, if for no other reason than there is not much to do sitting home alone in an apartment, even if it's only Thursday night.

But, at some point, I realize Cherry and I have had too much to drink for either of us to be concerned about whether or not we were working on our projects or whether or not my girlfriend was going to show up.

As if she were reading my mind, she blurts suddenly, "Well, my boyfriend won't be showing up, that's for sure." Cherry laughs out loud.

I wonder if maybe I spoke out loud about Toni. "Let's hope not! Actually, will they even let him in?"

"Bah, who knows. Who cares. He is off with his guy friends for poker night. They do that every month or two and he drinks too much, and smokes too much, and comes home all horny and aggressive."

"That's different from...?" I pretend to ask seriously, then laugh out loud as she starts to answer. She laughs with me.

Cherry stands and extends her hand to me. I am certain her eyes sparkle. "Come on, let's get out of here, I can't drink any more."

I don't think I should drink any more either, so it's a good time to leave.

The warmth of her smile captivates me. I wonder if I am imagining things, but there seems to be some hint of attraction in the way she is making eye contact. I take her hand and we walk together, out of the bar and into the wee hours of Friday morning.

Some hesitation tickles at me when she does not release my hand. We walk close together. Her hips swing playfully, and, I imagine, intentionally, and bump mine gently on every step.

It is like the two of us have known each other for ages, and not like we had spoken, really, for the first time tonight. Other than saying hello in class, and project-planning discussions with our shared advisor, I don't know that we have ever talked about anything.

I feel oddly detached from myself, and lost in these few moments, where it is quiet and calm and I walk hand in hand with a straight woman from my graduate program, like this was the most normal activity in the world.

We arrive at Cherry's apartment. She has not released my hand. I have not released hers. She pulls me close and leans in as if to give me a hug, the warmth of her breath brushing against my face, my lips, as she lowers her voice. My eyes rest on her lips.

"Do you want to come up?"

I shake my head, slightly, "I can't... I... just can't."

"This night could make things different, for both of us," she suggests, her breath — scented with alcohol and warm and close — offering me a nearly undeniable temptation.

I hold my head back from her.

I am positive she wants to kiss me.

I don't know if I want to kiss her.

Well. I do. But. I have Toni at home, and Cherry has some man in her life, maybe even home now, upstairs. She smiles mischievously at my tension. "I like women, too," she states.

"Oh." I am not sure what to say. "Um. I think I figured that part out." I feel some pull, from somewhere inside me, to just kiss her, and see.

But. Despite the exhaustion and the work and the pressure, I believe I am happy with Toni. And Cherry is straight. Or, mostly straight, I suppose. And in a relationship, and what use is a one-night stand anyway. There is probably a lesson-learned to be found here.

I shake off the trance. I ignore this attraction that is not just physical, maybe not *even* physical. and I step back from her. Common sense makes me step back from her. I don't know how common sense made it through all the alcohol in my system, but it did.

The touch of her hand against mine now sends an thread of discomfort through me. I try to pull it away, the line between willpower and this urge stretching thin as she holds on.

My voice feels like it cracks. "You have a, well, man... and I have a girlfriend and..."

She just smiles at me. Her eyes don't leave mine.

"I can't. This won't end well," I mutter, the truth bitter.

"Well, endings are overrated..." Her gaze locked onto mine, there is an entire conversation held in this silent language.

"I can't Cherry." The regret lingers in the back of my mouth. I tug my hand again, and she releases it. I step back. "I don't think it's a good idea to get into that... situation..." I know that some lines, once crossed, can't be uncrossed. "I don't think either of our partners would approve."

If she pulls me back toward her, if she steps toward me, if she licks her lips one more time, I will kiss her. I will go up with her. We will see what happens.

But she does not. "You're probably right. And we both had too much to drink." She turns to her door and digs out her building key. "I enjoyed the evening," she says as she slips through the door. It closes softly behind her.

When I reach home — after a side trip to the coffee shop near the subway closest to our apartment, where I sit and sip coffee until the sun begins to rise — Toni is asleep in our bed, and all I can do is take a deep breath of relief that she is there and I am here and tonight's — last night's — temptation was just a moment fuelled by alcohol and exhaustion and curiosity.

As I slip into bed without waking Toni, I ignore the weird mix of disappointment and relief over declining Cherry's offer.

TOO TIRED FOR DIALOGUE

I REST my head against the bus window. It bumps, sometimes gently, sometimes not so gently, with the potholes and the frequent stops and starts as the bus makes its way down through Thornhill, into North York proper, then finally, to the Eglington West subway where the public transit service will be more frequent and have fewer stops and starts.

I feel the tears prick my eyes. I force myself to ignore them, to erase them. I try to think about something happy, something distracting, but all I have room for just now, currently, here in Toronto, is work and study and 90 minute commutes each way to either, to both. It doesn't matter if I am going from home to work or work to campus or home to university, or, actually, anywhere at all, it takes 90 minutes. And, since I have to go to campus most days and to work all days, it is not unusual to spend four hours a day on public transit.

I am tired.

Exhausted.

I can barely believe Toni and I have been in Toronto for nearly four months now. Soon heading into the fifth, I realize. I make a mental note to check I will have the rent money for November. In a different situation, such as one where Toni never left Laurence and I was coming here to Toronto on my own, I would have waited until closer to the start of the school year before moving. But as it was, Toni and I headed up here shortly after Chris and I decided our sharing a one-bedroom when one of us had a frequent overnight guest who appeared to have more or less moved in but did not pay rent and the mattress she and I had been sleeping on took up the entire open side of the living room was not working anymore. I didn't disagree. The space had never really been big enough for two of us and it was totally inappropriate for three.

So, barely four weeks into our new, exciting, sex-in-every-corner relationship — our post-Laurence relationship — Toni and I headed off to Toronto.

My employer had put me through university — working part-time and flexible hours meant I was able to afford to live through the nearly five years it took me to graduate. My student loans were big, but I knew people who had much bigger ones, so the working-my-way through university was mostly successful. When I spoke to my boss about moving earlier than originally planned at the end of the summer, he contacted a colleague at a store in Thornton, just north of Toronto proper, and on the public transit line, so at least I had arrived with a job already lined up.

What I hadn't known at that time was that this job was a 90 minute commute from the only area in which I could both afford an apartment and feel safe living in that apartment.

Toronto is more expensive than I had realized, and my part-time job that put me through my undergraduate degree was not going to fund my way through graduate school. So I had to get a second job. Which made scheduling the new challenge. I had to find a second job with consistent and non-conflicting hours — which ended up being weekend overnights at a residential complex, as front desk security. I didn't mind the work, it was quiet and I was mainly just a presence on site for insurance purposes, which gave me time to do some of my class assignments, at least for a couple hours early into my shifts, before exhaustion made it impossible to read, or think.

The bus finally bumps into the alcove along the edge of the subway station and I make my way down the escalators. The place is quiet, it's nearly 9 p.m., but it's only Thursday so it is off-hours for workers, and for partiers. The subway, fortunately, still runs frequently but the bus service that just dropped me off, not so much. It runs only every 30 minutes this time of day, and it is not uncommon that the bus comes just enough minutes early that I miss the 8:10 that stops just outside the store where I work.

I get off the subway at the stop closest to my apartment and walk up the stairs to the street. There can be buses here sometimes, that will drop me off right in front of the apartment, but, if there is not — and tonight there is not — it is faster for me to walk the several blocks than to wait for the bus.

If I wasn't exhausted, with stingingly tired eyes, with a paper to complete for Monday, I might enjoy the walk. As it is, it is just another chore tacked onto my day and the tension that runs outward from my chest along my limbs makes it impossible to even think about the things I pass on the walk.

The things like that pile of garbage, out front of the store that sells the Jamaican patties that I often grab as quick and cheap meals on my way to the subway, those boxes stacked wet and topplely along that alleyway, the two women standing at the bus stop looking expectantly up the street, the series of buildings that, at some point, must have been storefronts for shoe stores and clothing boutiques and hardware shops which are now vacant and boarded and have nothing to look at in the windows.

The only businesses on this walk from the subway that are still in business are the Jamaican patty shop and a tiny Chinese food restaurant that has only the one table to sit at, but has a robust takeout clientele, both closed at this hour.

I let myself into the apartment. The lights at the bottom of the stairs, where the living area in this small one bedroom apartment is, are on.

"Hey, anyone home, it's Avon visiting."

I don't hear any response as I come down the stairs.

"Toni?"

I pop my head into the bedroom doorway, she isn't home.

I sit on the battered and covered-with-a-sheet rocker-recliner that we bought from a second hand store when we arrived and put my hands over my face. I had spoken to her earlier in the day, from work, and she had been planning to go job hunting in the afternoon.

"Bet you're having great luck finding work at this hour," I mutter to myself.

She had gotten a job within a week of our arrival, but left it after only a couple days because the boss was overbearing and she thought he was ogling her. And, the work was menial — cleaning office buildings. She found another a couple weeks after that, in security, similar to my weekend overnight job, but daytime, down-town, and for a different security company.

I had thought that was going well, and I was just getting settled in with my two job routine, and preparing for classes to start the first week of September, and looking forward to having enough income to be able to drop my overnight work, when she quit. They were unreasonable, she thought, because they had given her a formal reprimand for arriving late to her shift on a regular basis. She had explained that the bus-subway connection to get her downtown was the problem. She would have to leave home 30 minutes earlier to accommodate delays, and would end up being early most shifts, and they didn't pay her for arriving early. And, while she did still have her car, parking downtown cost too much to take the car.

She had been looking for work since.

I glance at the clock and head back to the bedroom to look out the window at the building parking area. The area is well-lit and is sort of a courtyard with low, two-story buildings around it. I never investigated what was in the buildings on the back side of the lot, but the neighboring one is an empty storefront building, like the others I walk by from the subway station. This space in the back of the buildings holds mainly building supply materials — the big stuff, so it's not likely to be stolen — and stacks of flattened cardboard. There are dumpsters, which always have things in them, but nothing that smelled, and we have been here all summer, so if something was going to smell, it would have. There is a space behind this building, directly outside our bedroom window, where two cars can fit. We use one of them and the other is intended for the upstairs neighbor, but they don't have a car, so it is always empty.

It is empty now too. Both spaces. Toni must have taken the car to whatever interview she had been heading to.

But she should have been home by now.

This is my only night off this week — actually, every week. I don't have class on Fridays and don't work again until Friday overnight.

I pick up the landline in the living room and call her. I still don't have a cell phone, I had been waiting for Toni to find work so she could pay toward the household expenses and rent before getting one. But the internet and television package still included a landline for some odd reason, and I still owned an old-fashioned corded phone, so old-school it is, for a little while longer.

The phone rings through to voice mail.

"Hey, Toni, where are you? I just got home."

I hang up and sit down in the rocker-recliner.

The phone ringing jolts me awake.

Startled — I hadn't realized I was sleeping — I grab it, "Hi?"

"Hey Liz. Just got your message. Am celebrating — I found a job today — a good one — I start next week... meant to call you before you left work but was driving and by the time I got stopped, you had already left to catch the bus."

A spiral of relief spikes through me. "What's the job?"

"I'll be working in an office. Days, and there is parking, so no need to worry about transit schedules... hey, anyway, why don't you come join me at Petals, I am here, having a celebratory drink..."

The thought of another public transit transportation nightmare 90 minutes almost makes me say no. But. She has been looking for a suitable job for weeks, and with money from this new job, scrounging up rent won't be quite as stressful, and, if it pays okay, maybe I can drop my overnight weekend job and live a normal-ish part-time worker, full-time student life sooner, rather than later, so it is definitely worth celebrating.

"I just got home so will change and head right out." Thinking through the routing to get downtown on public transit, I figure it's only going to take 45 minutes or so... "I should be about an hour."

"Great! See you then, love ya."

She disconnects before I have a chance to reply.

On the Road

LEARNING TO SWALLOW

IN THE KITCHEN I find the tequila bottle is already down on the counter, and there are two shot glasses and a salt shaker beside it. I check the fridge but there is no lemon. I take a tumbler from the cupboard and pour some tequila into it. I leave the bottle and the shot glasses on the counter and head to the washroom to wash my face and armpits. I pause and stare at myself in the mirror. Pits, tits, and slits — what my birth mother, when I was visiting her during her 2 weeks of summer custody — called a whore's bath.

We are estranged now, but, unlike with the rest of my family, the estrangement has nothing to do with my "choices", it is entirely related to her skipping off to someplace hot and sunny with her latest husband, who isn't a big fan of, well, her having contact with anyone other than him. If anything, she would have been the sole family member who wouldn't have batted an eye if I brought a girlfriend home. Before she married for this fourth, and latest, time, that is.

I walk back to the subway and head to Petals, one of the two women's bars in the city. Well, Petals is a bar — a nightclub — and the other, Sapphics, is more like a lounge. They have poetry readings and drag king shows. Petals is, well, a dance bar pick-up place. You drink, you dance, you see someone of the right attrac-

79

tion and you head home together, for the night. If you were going to see them again, that's when you'd meet at Sapphics, where you could have a conversation and take some time to get to know the person.

Thinking about my evening with Cherry here, I shake my head. Petals almost wove its one-night magic over a straight woman.

I hear muffled music coming out of Petals from a couple buildings away. I head down the short flight of stairs and don't stop at the coat check. There is no cover on Thursday, so the woman at the door, sitting on a stool, is looking at her phone and does not look up at me until I am past her and through the doorway into the bar, and then it's only a quick glance before returning to her phone.

There are a dozen or so tables to the left side of the square room, and a large dance floor along the other side of the table seating. The dance floor is partially enclosed with short walls, and the space between these walls, where people can move from the seating to the dancing areas, is a direct path to the front of the bar. Only the corners of the dance floor are not viewable from the tables, even if one had clear line of sight, which, on a Thursday night, one pretty much does.

I see Toni sitting at a table, watching people dancing on the other side of the short wall. There is a blond woman sitting with her. They are sitting very close to each other.

I do not stop at the bar on my way over. I know what Toni would drink, but don't know the blond woman, and don't want to join them with a solitary drink in hand. And I really don't want to be buying drinks for a stranger, at regular bar prices.

Toni sees me as I approach. She pushes her chair back and stands up, smiling. I wonder if her speed in standing had something to do with her, and the blond woman's, hands being under the table.

Toni hugs me and kisses beside my ear, before stepping back and introducing us, "Jackie, this is Liz. Liz... Jackie."

Jackie sticks her hand out, but does not stand, "Glad to meet you."

I shake her hand. Her grip is limp, and it almost seems like she placed her hand on top of mine as if she expected me to lift it to my lips and kiss it.

There is no chair on Toni's side of the table, so I sit beside Jackie. Toni sits back down in her seat, with Jackie sitting between us. The music is loud and it's hard to hear Toni when she says something to Jackie.

Jackie smiles at me and pushes her chair back, "Any preference? I'm going to the bar."

I shake my head and slide over into her seat as soon as she turns away. "Toni, what the hell?"

"She's my new boss."

"What? Doing what?"

"She is an interior designer, has her own business, and needs someone to help out, mainly in the office, but also when she stages places."

"And, what does she expect you to be doing? Testing out the beds?"

Toni just looks at me.

"Okay, okay, sorry... this is just... surprising. That you just found someone, out of the blue, who not only has a job for you, but that you could meet here at a women's dance bar..."

"I met her last weekend. You were working."

This surprises me. "You were out last weekend? Where did you meet her? You hadn't mentioned her."

"Actually, I met her at Sapphics." Before I can even raise my eyebrow, she continues, "I was there to see if they were hiring, door or coat check or something. Jackie was there, heard me asking the bartender about work, and said she might be able to find something."

"Oh?" I watch Jackie make her way back to the table, three drinks held awkwardly between her hands.

Toni sees me looking and practically jumps out of her seat to rush over to meet Jackie. She takes one of the drinks and returns to place it in front of me. I don't move out of "her" seat, so Jackie leans between Toni and I and sets a drink on the table, before taking the remaining drink and sitting to my left.

"Got you a margarita. Toni tells me they're your favorite." Jackie's thin delicate lips form a fake smile.

"She tells you, huh... that part of the job interview? What your girlfriend drinks?" I don't even try to refrain from sounding snarky.

Jackie makes eye contact with Toni. I see Toni's smile, and recognize these are real smiles on both their faces. Nothing like the polite one Jackie has for me.

I pick up my glass and hold it out. "Well, then, cheers to new 'jobs,'" and down the drink without waiting for either of them to get their glasses up to clink.

* * *

It is mid afternoon before I am awake. The night before is a blur. I don't actually recall getting home, but it must have been after the bar closing, and on the night bus. I glance out the window and see that the car is there. This is surprising, since Toni doesn't drive drunk, and I am pretty sure I wasn't drinking alone.

But, maybe I was. The blur doesn't come clear enough for me to know.

Toni is in the living room, sitting on the couch, a coffee in front of her, her phone in her hands.

"Morning," I say.

She doesn't look up, "Afternoon."

I walk past her and into the kitchen where I pour myself a hair-of-the-dog from the tequila bottle that is still sitting on the counter. I use the same glass I used last night — one less dish to wash.

* * *

"You're working all weekend."

"Yes, but..."

She cuts me off. "You work all the time, you're gone all weekend, and when you get home, you just want to sleep."

I feel the heat rise into my face. "You don't work at all. We have to pay rent."

She looks at me with her big sad eyes. "That's not fair. I found a job."

"Did you? Is that a job, following Jackie around all weekend?"

"This weekend is a conference she is going to. I am just joining her to see what she does at them. I don't want to sit around here and watch you sleep!"

I can't understand Toni's... presumption... her inability to appreciate why I might find it unacceptable for her to go away for the weekend with her soon-to-be new boss. "Toni. Seriously? You think I should be okay with you spending the weekend with another woman?"

"I am just going to learn the job. And I will be working with her directly, so we need to get to know each other..."

"So, you're not attracted to her?"

She just looks at me in response. I know that look. I don't take any comfort in knowing that she isn't going to lie to me — this isn't because she can't, or doesn't want to, but because she probably doesn't see why she might have to.

"You're always working, or sleeping, or too tired. We haven't had sex in weeks."

I feel queasy in my chest, panic is slipping up through me. I am tired. I am working too much. She is correct — I have not had the energy, or the time, for sex in weeks. The handful of late night quickies to satisfy her before I pass out from exhaustion does not count.

"I don't know what you want me to say Toni."

"I just want to go for the weekend, have some fun, meet some new people. I don't want to sit in this dump..." she opens her arms to indicate the apartment we share.

"And, will you be having sex with her?" The question I don't want to ask, don't want to know the answer to, comes out anyway. I swallow a mouthful of my drink while I wait for her answer.

"It would just be sex. I love you Liz. I am just lonely. And need to have some fun, to enjoy life, this isn't doing that for me. It doesn't mean I care any less about you."

And, there is the crux of my worry, my concern, my "issue" with her going away for the weekend. I am not emotionally able to accept that her having sex with another woman does not reflect on how she feels about me. Monogamy has been well-trained in me. It might be serial, but it is still, mostly, monogamous.

"That doesn't work for me..." I can't even find the words.

"Okay, what if I agree to not have sex with Jackie, but just go and enjoy the weekend away, and learn my new job, which will help us, right?"

I finish my drink and set the glass down on the coffee table. I head to the bedroom. "I have to get ready for work," I pause in the doorway and look at her. She is still standing in the living room, near the doorway to the stairs. "You will have to choose, Toni, I am not going to be the little-woman sitting home waiting for you to come back after your weekend away having "fun" It's not even the sex, it's the... attraction... you have for her. There's something wrong between us, and screwing her, or wanting to screw her but refraining from it because I asked you to, won't fix that."

"Liz. You know me better than that. You know what I'm like." Toni almost whines.

I do. I do know her better than that. I know her only too well. If I were to be honest with myself, I would have to admit I knew her *too well* from the very first moment I heard her speak to her girlfriend on the phone while she practically had her hand down my pants in a public washroom.

But I don't want to admit that.

I am dressed in my uniform for my Friday overnight shift by the time I hear the apartment door clunk closed. I watch out the window as her feet pass in front of it on her way to get into her car.

I make myself a fresh drink and drink it quickly, while I force myself to think about what research paper reading I will take with me to work so I can get something done while sitting at the security desk all night. That would be a better use of my limited wakeful hours than thinking about Toni.

Then I head out to wait for the bus, for my 90 minute commute to my overnight shift in an apartment complex.

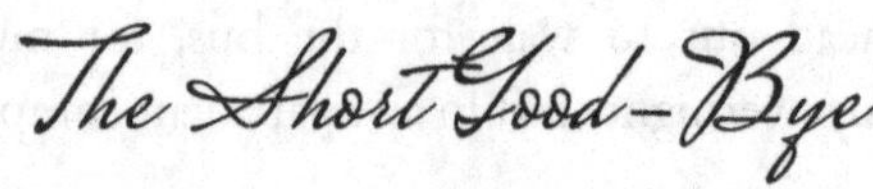

The Short Good-Bye

TONI TAKES her final box of personal items up the stairs and out to the car. I remain in the living room. I am surprised when she comes back down.

"Forget something?"

"Liz," she stands in the middle of the living room, "I want to say goodbye... I love you."

I finish my drink and set the glass down before looking up at her, "Okay, goodbye."

"Can I get a hug?"

A wave of anger sends a rush up my chest. "Is this how it went with Lo when you left her? Sorry, not sorry, but I found a new piece and I gotta go. But I love you, now gimme a hug?"

I see tears well in her eyes. "That's not fair. I can't help that I get lonely. And I don't want to leave you, this was your choice. You kicked me out, remember?"

She is not incorrect. When I got home from work on Saturday morning, there was a note on the coffee table. The "job offer" was too good for Toni to pass up, and she felt she had to go to the conference with Jackie to secure it. Oh, and she loved me and didn't plan on cheating and we could talk about it when she was back on Monday.

And then she didn't get back until Wednesday.

But she did leave me a voice mail to let me know she was okay — Jackie had added a couple extras days to the trip so she could network with colleagues in Montreal, and because Toni's spoke French, she was going to assist. On salary too.

I am home when she returns late Wednesday evening. She breezes in and takes her suitcase to the bedroom and drops it beside the bed, and flops down on it. "I am exhausted," she states as I follow her into the bedroom.

I don't remind her that I am also exhausted. That today alone I spent four hours on public transit, commuting between home and campus and campus and work and work and home. That my day started at 6 a.m., and I had just gotten home 20 minutes ago, and I am so tired I want to cry and I am so disappointed I want to cry, and I am so exhausted that I can't even respond to her claim of exhaustion. I am zombified with exhaustion.

I want to let it go. I want to just carry on and pretend Toni never went away *for work* for five days, like it is perfectly acceptable, and innocent. But, I don't let it go. I can't let it go. I understand that some people have different types of romantic attachments. I am aware that that exists.

But I don't understand *how* that exists.

I am betrayed.

I don't understand how Toni can claim to love me, or think that she respects me, if she is cheating on me with someone else.

What goes around comes around, Liz.

There is a small, tiny, delicate sliver of hope that exists in the handful of moments before I ask the question. The only question that can be asked, the question I must ask, even though I am nearly certain I do not want to hear the answer I am nearly certain I know I am going to hear.

"Did you fuck her?"

Toni, whose eyes had closed, opens them again and sits up against the wall where a headboard should be, but the bed frame is a cheap metal wheeled one from a local second-hand shop and doesn't have a headboard. "It wasn't like that, Liz. We talked about this. It's only sex, it didn't mean anything." She tries to take my hand, "I love you."

And so it ends. I sleep on the couch that night and, before leaving for campus on Thursday ask Toni to be sure she was moved out by the end of the day.

She is not there on Thursday evening when I get home, but there are a few boxes of her things stacked in the corner in the bedroom. Three boxes of things. The sum of our romance is three. I giggle to myself and finish off the bottle of tequila she did not pack.

And here it is, Friday early afternoon, and Toni is picking up the last of her things. I wonder why she didn't come when she knew I wouldn't be home. Fridays are my day off, at least until the overnight shift. She could have come this evening, and had the place to herself while she removed herself from the place. So she wanted this confrontation.

Probably, to her, it's not a confrontation, it's a resolution.

She is still standing there, presumably waiting for a hug, when I go into the kitchen and look through the cupboards to find something to make myself a drink. I am popping the last two ice cubes out of the tray when I hear the door at the top of the stairs clunk closed. When I come back out to the living room, Toni's keys are on the coffee table.

I call in sick to work. They ask if I am certain I won't be able to make it in, the work isn't strenuous, and I can ask my colleague in the opposite building to do all the patrols. It will be difficult for them to find a replacement on such short notice, especially for the overnight. Nobody wants to work a Friday overnight.

I don't blame them. I don't want to work a Friday overnight. But I insist I am much too ill to make it in to work. And that I hope I will be feeling better in time for Saturday night's shift, and will let them know as soon as possible.

I have called the only other lesbian I know in Toronto. She is also from back home but has lived in Toronto since after high school. I had met her through a local bootlegger, when we both wanted to get into the local gay bar. The two of us were underage and used very badly made fake id, from this bootlegger guy, to get into the bar. The bartender didn't look very closely, and, once we had been in the first time, we were never asked for id again. It was a small town, with a small gay bar, and, I think, the bartender had a soft spot for troubled young lesbians who were looking for a place to hang out where they weren't being pressured into hetero-sexuality.

Sierra and I weren't friends. And we never really hung out, other than that first night, on our first entry into the gay bar, which, to us, was the entrance to the gay world, at a time when we only peripherally knew it existed, and neither of us were out in our day-to-day lives.

I wasn't really in, just was never really out either. It wasn't something I ever talked about. I didn't need to. My family pretty much ignored my... attractions... thinking it was just a phase I would eventually grow out of — once I got over my rebellious stage and realized I wanted the husband and children and white picket fence.

Sierra, however, was strictly closeted. Her family would have kicked her out to live on the street if she had ever come out to them. So, when she finally did come out to them, it was on her way to the bus station, suitcase of belongings in hand, to begin her new, lesbian, life in Toronto.

I never knew her very well, and certainly don't know anything of her life here, now, but... she is literally the only non-work and non-university related phone number I have for someone in the city. Well, other than Toni.

So, I called Sierra and blabbered out the short story of what happened and asked what she was doing this weekend because I needed some distraction from sitting alone in my apartment and dwelling on all the things that had just gotten worse with Toni's departure. Not only was I alone in the city, but now there wasn't even a hope for Toni, someone, anyone, to help pay the bills, or to assist with the household activities such as laundry and grocery shopping.

I am sinking with the overwhelm.

I don't know that I can do this anymore.

She seemed happy to hear from me, though not happy for me, given the circumstances. She said she had a new girlfriend, from England, who had just recently arrived in Toronto and they had been planning to go out tonight anyway. They would go to Petals instead of Sapphics and would meet me there around 10.

She had laughed when she said I would have more luck at Petals as that's where all the single girls went to pick up. "You heard of hair of the dog... well, Petals will be like hair of the girl for you."

I go to the Jamaican patty shop in the early evening, to pick up some beer. There is nothing left to drink in the apartment, and the liquor store is a bus ride away, so I have to settle for beer. As I stumble my way back down the stairs into my apartment, I realize it is probably a good idea to switch over to beer... it is still hours before I am to meet Sierra — and her new British girlfriend — at Petals and I should try to be somewhat coherent when I get there.

When I get there, I am somewhat coherent. I am 40 minutes early, intentionally. The outrageous $20 cover charge starts at 10 p.m. and I don't see the need to pay for the privilege of entering a bar, when the money will be much better spent on drinks while I am in there.

I pop down the stairs and pass the coat check and the door person without pausing. The door person is the same woman from last week — was it only a week ago that this all came tumbling down? Oh, 8 days, so, more than week — but she does not have her phone out.

The place is no busier than it was last week when I met Toni and Jackie here. A couple tables with a couple people sitting, a half dozen dancers, nobody at the bar. I head to the bar where there are stools lined up in a neat row. I choose one at the end, toward the wall. The bartender smiles and asks what I'll be having.

When my Long Island comes, I turn my back to the bar and watch the handful of dancers.

WHAT IF THE DOOR DOES HIT YOUR ASS ON THE WAY OUT?

I AM STANDING at the bar, paying for my third Long Island when someone slips their arms around my waist and leans into me and whispers into my ear while bumping hips into my ass. "What's a girl like you doing in a nice place like this?"

I don't enjoy the hip bumping, or the whispering in my ear, but I smile as I turn to face my groper. Sierra has shown up to keep me company, changing her plans with her new girlfriend, so I can't begrudge her her entertainment. I expect she is showing off for the new girlfriend.

The new girlfriend is standing beside Sierra, facing away from the bar, and swaying to the music. Sierra orders drinks for them.

I don't hear what she orders because her girlfriend has turned back toward us and my pulse is rushing in my ears.

Her eyes, eyes the exact color of mine, meet mine. The world moves into slow motion. I watch her as her lips turn up into a smile and her eyes... absorb me. She leans forward and puts out her hand, "Heya. Sierra's rude. I'm Glen."

I take her hand. I feel my palm turn sticky with sweat even before it connects with hers. A tingle shoots down my neck and my armpits prickle. Her hand is dry and warm and firm and she grips mine solidly, for a second, then lets it go and leans back and tilts her head toward the dance floor, "Love this music, I'm going to dance." And she heads off to the dance floor.

My hand is tingling. Hot. I imagine I can still feel her grip on it. Holding it. Dry and warm and firm. I think the press of her hand has imprinted on my skin. The press of her eyes have imprinted on my face.

I watch her walk, dance, sway, her way to the dance floor. She doesn't look back at us. Sierra steps up beside me, a drink in each hand. "And... she's off..." She sips the drink in her left hand and lifts her right to point in the general direction of an empty table that has a clear view of the dance floor. "She'll be a while, dancing."

We sit. The bar is still pretty quiet, but it's not even 10:30. The dance floor has a small cluster of people, and Glen, off on her own, swaying to the music, facing away from us toward the DJ. As we watch, another woman joins Glen, says something to her, then starts dancing with her.

As the surprise wave of jealousy spins through me, I glance at Sierra, who has her glass to her lips and the straw in her mouth. She is watching the dance floor as well, but with a smile.

"She likes to dance."

"It seems so." I try to restrain myself from asking, but cannot. "How did you meet? She's from... England you said? Were you there?"

Sierra laughs, "Not yet, no, but I will go there. Maybe sooner rather than later too... I have actually always wanted to. I met Glen here. Two weeks ago. Believe it or not, this is the place to go when you have a broken heart." She winks at me.

"Broken heart?" I try to think through this logic. "Whose heart was broken?"

Sierra literally guffaws. "Ch'anié ... turns out both of ours. She had just arrived from England — she's from some place outside of Manchester. Some small village. I don't remember its name: Kington or Stoneton or something like that, with a -ton at the end." She leans toward me, conspiratorially, "I think all their villages end in 'ton, by the sounds of it."

I want her to get back to how they met. I am interested in Glen, not in a geography lesson. I am about to tell her that... well, the second part of that, when she continues.

"You're not going to believe this. This is why it's ch'anié — kismet. Glen arrived in Toronto on Tuesday, two weeks ago — two weeks and a few days ago now, I guess. She and her chick in Manchester, wherever, split up and she came to Canada, to Toronto, to clear her head. I was here, on Friday night because Jackie had just dumped me, the weekend before and I needed to clear my own head." She grins at me, "Or find someone to help me get over Jackie, more like."

The name jolts me. Toronto is a big city, and the women's spaces are few, so the name might just be coincidence.

But. How common is Jackie, really.

"How long were you and Jackie together?" I don't know why I care.

I don't care. I just need to make small talk to keep my mind off Glen's dancing and the additional woman who has joined her and the first woman on the dance floor.

And off Jackie. Off all Jackies.

"Over a year. We didn't fight much either, so it was a bit of a surprise. But she met someone, so... I was old news. Went from 'all is normal' to, 'it's time we went our separate ways', all in the same weekend."

"Who did she meet?" A knot of tension swells in my stomach. I know the answer. I ask anyway.

Sierra shrugs. "Some French woman, here. It was like some bad movie. She goes out Friday night — though I guess I should have known something was up — we often hang with a group of friends and had an escape room planned for Friday, and she didn't want to go — meets some French woman here, then two days later kicks me to the curb."

"This was three weekends ago?"

"Yup... then, like some miracle, Glen walks into my life the week after." Sierra finishes her drink, nods at my empty glass and pushes her chair back from the table, "Be back in a couple, keep an eye on my girl for me, okay?" She chuckles as she heads to the bar.

My eyes return to Glen, who has now gotten half the dance floor dancing with her. "I don't mind at all." I speak out loud, but Sierra is out of hearing range now.

* * *

Glen eventually makes her way back to us at the table, "You squares don't dance?" She is shiny with sweat. She plops into the chair beside Sierra and picks up the drink in front of Sierra. Sierra has finished the drink she brought for Glen, ages ago, and has just the one drink in front of her now.

"Can't dance, can't sing, too fat to fly," I smile at her.

She looks from my face, down my chest, to where the table blocks her view of the rest of me. "Don't know about the singing or dancing, yet, but pretty sure you could fly."

I feel the flush start from my feet and move upward.

Sierra puts her arm around Glen. "Are you sitting for a while? Do you want a drink?"

Glen doesn't stop looking at me. "Yes."

Sierra stands, kisses the top of Glen's head and walks back to the bar.

Glen still watches me. "You've known Sierra long?"

"From back home, yes, but I haven't seen her in years. I just moved to Toronto this summer, for university, she's been here for years... we never really kept in touch. Just on social media, which neither of us seem to use much..." I cut off my babbling.

"Canada is lovely."

"I don't know that Toronto is representative of Canada though, have you been elsewhere?"

She smiles and I feel my face get hot — get hotter. "Not yet.

But I hope to make enough friends that I might visit other areas, with them."

I imagine her foot under the table, bumping against my own.

I am not imagining it.

I stare at her, lost in her eyes, my eyes, on her. Her eyes on me. My head is woozy. It must be the alcohol.

Sierra sits between us.

Glen's foot stops rubbing against my leg, but I don't see her shift in her seat. She picks up her glass, "To Canader, eh?"

Sierra clinks her glass on each of ours, "To Petals, may it bring Liz the pleasure it has brought us!"

I smile. And wonder how might it bring me the exact pleasure it brought Sierra... the identical exact one...

I don't have my own cheer to make.

* * *

The bartender's last call bell was a while ago. We have finished our last round of drinks. The music has ended, the lights have been getting progressively brighter and are now on full.

"All right ladies. Get out." The door person, now bouncer, points the broom in her hands toward the door.

They have to be direct. Their subtle hints have not broken the flow of conversation among us. Between us, actually. Sierra is just listening. Glen and I are talking. I am learning about her travels, why she is here in Canada, what her plans are for the future.

Sierra listens, with her arm wrapped possessively around Glen, her chair turned out, tucked against Glen's chair, both of them facing me across the table.

Almost simultaneously Glen and I push our chairs out from the table, Sierra looks like she nearly loses her balance, but pops up on her feet just a second behind Glen and I. I think she might have been asleep.

"You alright, Sierra?" I ask as she knocks the chair over. Glen catches it before it clatters on the floor. The door person, come bouncer, huffs. She says something but I don't catch the words. I am watching Glen right the chair and tuck her arm into Sierra's. Glen is watching me as she does this.

"Rightio, off we go." Glen tugs Sierra's arm and they move toward the exit.

I walk behind them. I scramble to think of a way to prolong this evening, this night. Or to extend it through tomorrow. And the next day? And the one after that?

And Glen figures it out for me. "Liz. I think you should come with us. It's too late to be going alone on the night bus... all sorts of drunks on there."

Sierra giggles, then hiccups loudly. Then burps.

"You're so rude, Sierra."

Sierra burps again. And laughs out loud. "You're so prim, Glen. Must be the Brit in you," she guffaws and burps even more loudly. "I'll show you rude," and she smacks Glen on the butt, "when we get home."

I step forward and realize I am about to grab Sierra's arm and... twist it, break it, make it stop smacking, touching, holding, Glen...

I stop myself, and, instead, slip between the two of them, an arm around each waist, "Don't mind if I do."

Dark Roast Coffee

Sierra's apartment is cute and modern. She has a one bedroom only a couple blocks past the Dundas subway stop. I don't ask what her rent is. I also don't ask what she does for a living to be able to afford what this rent must be. Partly because she is quite drunk and is a splattery drunk — almost slobbery — and she isn't able to hold herself upright on a couch, let alone make coherent conversation, and partly because I don't want to encourage her to join Glen and I in conversation.

After depositing Sierra on the couch, where she slides downward and tips sideways, looking uncomfortable but not complaining, Glen and I sit at the tall dining table which is directly behind the couch. The open kitchen area — which is really just a wall with a small stove, huge fridge and regular size microwave, with a sink in the corner at the end — is separated from the living room space by a narrow island.

Running along the wall beside us is a staircase to a railed loft that makes the ceiling of the living room and opens above our heads at the dining table. The railing above us makes a left where the island is, and runs the length of the kitchen and bathroom, creating an L-shaped second floor.

"Coffee?" Glen has barely been seated before she pops up from her seat, walks to the kitchen and pulls an electric kettle from a cupboard on the far side behind the kitchen island. I nod, but she isn't looking. She fills the kettle, plugs it in, and retrieves a French press from the same place she got the kettle. She free-pours some pre-ground coffee from a Starbucks bag into it, then leans her elbows on the island, puts her hands under her chin and props her head on them, facing me.

"I love Starbucks."

I do as well. "It's American. We have Tim Horton's." I sound so dumb. "I mean, obviously we have both, just, Tim's is Canadian."

I think, for a second, to correct myself, "Tim's *was* Canadian. It isn't now, hasn't been for... some time..." but I am certain she doesn't care. I know I don't.

She nods at me. "Yes."

We stare at each other. The minutes pass.

The kettle starts whistling quietly.

Glen pours the water over the coffee grinds and takes two mugs from a cupboard beside the fridge. She hooks them over her fingers and carries the French press and mugs over to the table and sets them down. "There is no milk. Sierra's lactose intolerant."

"What do you do, at home, in England?"

"I manage a pub. Well, assist in the managing of a pub, more like." She shrugs, "Right now I am taking a break."

"For how long? ummm... how long are you thinking of staying in Canada, or, Toronto?"

My eyes. I mean, my eyes in her, watch me. I know eyes can't twinkle, but they do. Mischievously, it seems. "I don't know. My return ticket is mid November."

Something surges into my throat and I can't speak for a second. "That's only, like, three weeks!"

She doesn't comment on how desperate I sound. "Just over, yeah. I didn't know I would meet Sierra when I planned my trip. I thought more than five or six weeks would have been too long. That's a long time to be living out of youth hostels."

"Oh, you're staying at the hostel?"

She laughs. "No. I am staying here, now. I met Sierra in my first week in the country and haven't gotten anywhere, other than the bar, yet. Oh, well, I did go up the CN Tower, and walked the Islands, though there weren't any bathers at Hanlan Point."

That makes sense. Summer season was over long before she arrived. The beach and park destinations in October would not have been very busy. She should have come in the summer.

I should have met her in the summer.

I should have met her before I even moved here, with Toni...

All the things that could have happened. But never did.

I slowly push the coffee plunger down. "So you were here for Thanksgiving? That's the weekend you met Sierra?"

"Kind of. We, obviously, don't have Thanksgiving in the UK. So that wasn't really a thing I even thought of. And, well, Sierra is Dene. So Thanksgiving isn't really a thing for her. Well, not a thing to celebrate anyway."

I hadn't thought of either of those realities. Of course the UK wouldn't celebrate Thanksgiving, at least not in the UK... and neither would many of the indigenous nations in North America. Thanksgiving is probably an exclusively in-colony celebration. "Oh my fuck... I never even thought of that..." I am actually a bit baffled at my ignorance.

I pour our coffees. Both are black.

I don't mention that I also didn't celebrate Thanksgiving because I was working at double time and a half instead. I needed the money more than I needed to eat turkey with my girlfriend. Not that I could have afforded turkey anyway.

And now that she is my ex-girlfriend, I am especially relieved that I had swapped the holiday for the money.

My hand is cupped around my coffee mug. Glen moves her cup closer until it is close enough for her to tilt and click against mine, "To the end of colonization."

I can feel the heat from her fingers, or her cup, perhaps.

I take a sip of coffee. "Cheers to the end of colonization." The moment feels surreal.

Sierra jerks upward in her seat and grunts, "What's up?"

"I was just chatting with our imperial colonizer here." I don't take my eyes off Glen.

Glen laughs.

Sierra levers herself off the couch with the arm of the Queen Anne chair beside it. When she has her footing, she notices the French press, "Hey, is there more coffee?"

She can see that the press is nearly empty. Glen raises her eyebrows at me and pushes back her chair, "I'll make some more."

Glen takes the press and heads over to the sink, Sierra watches her, then slowly and deliberately makes her way past the dining area toward the bathroom. "Gotta piss so bad," she mutters as she minces by.

I sip my coffee. And watch Glen as she waits for the kettle to boil again. It doesn't take as long this time. The water is still pretty warm, I guess. Sierra is banging around in the bathroom, but it doesn't sound like a fall-over and the noise doesn't repeat, so neither Glen nor I call out to ask if she's okay in there.

Glen returns to the table with a newly filled press and one mug this time. She sets them both down on the dining table and sits. "Molly Maid at your service."

"That's, ahh, a cleaning company, not a barista company."

"Right you are. No worries then. Molly Barista, at your service."

Sierra bursts out of the bathroom. "You bitches didn't even check I was okay."

"Were you okay?" I ask, my eyes wide.

"Yes."

"Oh, excellent." I finish my coffee. Sierra stands there and looks at us at the table. Glen presses down the press and pours coffee into the new mug, then fills mine. The little bit left, she pours into her own mug.

Sierra turns abruptly and heads up the stairs, "I'm going to bed."

She gets about four steps up before stopping. "Glen, are you coming?" Her tone is belligerent.

"Yes luv. I am coming, shortly."

Sierra huffs and carries on up the stairs. Glen finishes the rest of her coffee. "You can't sleep on that couch," she nods at the couch. She is correct, it is modern and has gaps between the three seat cushions, which aren't really cushions, just hard round pads. "That thing looks like an airport bench, minus the rails between the seats, and is about as comfortable. And I have dozed on enough airport benches to know."

"You hang out in airports a lot then?" I smile at her.

"Yeah, well, enough. England's not like here, visiting a neighboring country isn't an all day event. You guys drive longer to go to a neighboring city in the same province than it takes me to fly to Paris."

"I always wanted to go to Paris," I mutter.

"Go. What's keeping you here?" Glen asks, honestly.

"That's the million dollar question, isn't it. I have some sort of responsibility to finish graduate school and get a good job and settle down... I dunno." I suddenly feel bleak. And wish I had the nerve to ask if they had anything I could add to my coffee.

"Right. Well, that's not a question we can dig into at," she looks at her watch, "4 a.m. C'mon, go to the loo, and come to bed. You'll fit just fine in Sierra's king, we'll just have to snuggle close."

I don't think too deeply about this plan. I go to the washroom and wait at the bottom of the stairs for Glen to finish her turn in there. She comes out wearing only her underpants. Her shirt and pants are both folded in her hands. I assume her bra is folded with her other clothes. From what I can see, now, she likely doesn't go without a bra very often. Her breasts are firm and pert and large and milky white and, I bite the inside of my cheek and look away from her dark nipples, contracted in the cool air, I assume.

"Sierra won't find this weird?"

"Nah, she'll be passed out. Worst case, she'll wake up for a minute, have a little snog on me, and pass out again."

I don't think about the little snog part.

The loft is wide open and the bed is in the middle of the room, against the back wall of the apartment. Sierra is, indeed, sound asleep, lying on her side, facing the stairs, her arm draped off the edge of the bed. Glen goes around to the other side and climbs in. She slides over to nearly the middle of the bed.

"I assume you don't want the middle... you might get the snogging," she whisper-giggles.

It's definitely not Sierra's snogging I might want. But I don't say this.

I unbutton my jeans and slide them off, glad I didn't pick up Toni's habit of going commando. I pull off my top. I don't have a bra on, just a camisole, which I leave on. I am not quite as free with my nudity as Glen seems to be.

She is lying there, facing toward me, her arm tucked under her head. There is no pillow in the middle, just the one under Sierra's head, and the one on this side. I push it toward her, and she slips the end of it between her arm and her head.

I lie down, rigid, as close to the edge of the bed as I can, facing her. My head is on the other end of the king pillow and we are staring at each other, with our bodies separated. She slides her top arm across the space and walks her fingers up my belly to my side, just below my ribs. She digs her fingers in gently and tugs, urging me to move closer.

"You'll fall out, silly," she whispers, breathy. Her breath smells like dark coffee and a hint of alcohol.

It's warm. I'm warm. From my groin to my cheeks, I am flushed. I slide my hips closer, my torso, her hand remains draped over my side. Sierra snores indelicately on the far side of the bed.

I gaze into Glen's eyes.

She gazes back.

We fall asleep like that.

The Problem with Technology

GLEN and I are at a Starbucks just a block and a half from Sapphics. I have a date, in 45 minutes, with a woman I met through a dating app.

I don't know why I let Glen talk me into this. I put the tiny bottle of gin back into my jacket pocket and replace the lid on the coffee. "Glen. I don't know why I let you talk me into this."

She pats my non coffee holding hand, "Because you wanted to be talked into it. A lovely lass like yourself shouldn't be wallowing around single."

"I don't have time for this though. That's why my last relationship didn't work out — I am never around enough. I work too much," I repeat to her what I was told. I know it is the truth, but... why did I have to work too much? Was that my choice? If Toni had gotten a job, one that didn't involve having sex with her new boss, I mean, would I have had to work all the time?

Glen pinches the back of my hand. "Stop wallowing. Life is too short!"

"Can you read my mind?" I ask her, outright.

"Yes. I know you're feeling sorry for yourself. Now, go out there, go get 'er tigress! This Violet might be exactly what you're looking for..." she pauses and stares at my face, her eyes shifting back and forth on mine, "a sugar momma!"

She leans back in her chair and laughs.

I don't know if I find it as funny as she does. I don't know if I like the flicker of agreement that runs through me, for just a second, before I pinch that thought off, completely.

I finish my coffee and set the empty cup in the middle of the table. Glen tells me she will be staying for a while, for some quiet time away from Sierra, who is in a bit of a rage this evening because Glen didn't make anything for supper. Instead of arguing over why she didn't cook supper and have it ready on the table for Sierra's 5 p.m. arrival home after a hard day's work, Glen had phoned me and suggested we meet for coffee ahead of my date with Violet.

"Since you didn't do your wifely duties and cook supper, you can at least practice cleaning up — start with my coffee cup."

She rolls her eyes. "You're not my wife. Oh, wait, neither is Sierra. So piss off."

I ignore the tingle that runs through me.

* * *

Sapphics has quiet music playing and a low murmur of conversation in the background. I see a woman who looks like a slightly older, slightly stockier version of the online pictures of the woman I am meeting — Violet — sitting at the bar when I come in.

As I approach the bar, I hear her and the bartender having a conversation — about snow removal, apparently.

I interrupt them. "Hi, Violet? I'm Liz. we, ahh, met..."

The conversation with the bartender stops instantly, mid-sentence, and Violet pops off the stool. She has to look up at me. She sticks her hand out and I take it. "Nice to meet you. I got here early, to make sure I wasn't late. What do you want to drink? Sue here can make anything. I like her Slings the best, but I do like pineapple a lot. Want a Sling?" As I nod, she carries on, "Sue, two

Slings please, and can you take them to our table." She sweeps her arm to the right and I step in that direction, not sure which table she means to be ours.

She leads the way to a table in a corner, as far from the bar as we could be, and pulls out a chair. For me. She stands behind the chair expectantly, so I sit in it, and scoot my feet as she pushes it in. She sits across from me.

"Guess I can't pull yours out for you, huh," I joke.

She looks at me seriously, "Why would you?"

I shrug, "Just making conversation. This is my first, ah, blind date? Or app date? Not really sure if this is the same as a blind date."

"No. Blind date would indicate we met through a mutual friend. I don't think we have any mutual friends, well, I don't have any that know you. Do you know someone who knows me?" She peers at me.

"No, not at all." I wonder how to change the direction of this nonsense conversation. I wonder why I am even here, trying to have this conversation — is it too late to escape?

Violet doesn't seem to notice anything odd.

"Your profile said you were 24. Was that true? You don't really look 24. And you're still in university? Are you really 24? People sometimes lie about their ages." She hums, "Well, true, it's usually lying when they are older, to be younger, not the other way around." She takes a small breath, "I didn't post my age. I didn't want people to think age matters. I am 35, next week actually. On Tuesday, I turn 35."

The bartender shows up at the table with our drinks. I am relieved for the interruption. I put the straw to my lips as Violet gives the bartender a $50 and tells her she doesn't need any change.

Once the bartender leaves, Violet watches me sip my drink without saying anything.

I assume this means it is my turn to make small talk. "What do you do for a living?"

Her expression doesn't change. "I am a heavy equipment operator. For the government. I drive, well, snowplows soon. Gotta keep the roads clear. This time of year — from spring onward, really — it's mostly roadwork equipment, you know pavers, graders... whatever, for the job we're on. Until the snow comes, of course."

I am not sure how to hold up my end of this conversation. Or, more accurately, how I can pretend I want to. So I sip my drink and listen while Violet tells me about her job driving heavy equipment among the boys who treat her like one of the guys and she is grateful for that. There isn't much attitude from the regulars, but apparently some of the seasonal hires, sometimes, make comments to the other guys, within her hearing. She figures this is intentional passive-aggressive behavior because driving heavy equipment is a man's job, not meant for a four and a half foot woman.

"I am only four and a half feet tall, you know."

"Oh?" I am not sure if she thinks she looks taller, or that I can't guesstimate height because height is measured in numbers and I'm just a silly little girl.

The bartender miraculously appears with fresh drinks for us both. I didn't see Violet order them, but maybe I had blanked out — or dozed off — for a second while she was telling me about driving heavy equipment and she had waved the bartender over like her own personal wait staff. I smile at the bartender and say thanks. I am very glad to have a drink, with a straw I can suck in lieu of talking.

Violet gives the bartender another $50 and resumes her job description.

I don't really listen. I don't know that I nod or smile in the correct places, but I don't think Violet notices. She has a lot of work stories to share and seems to be on a mission to do just that. I wonder if I am her first date in a while.

"Have you been using the app long?" I wait until there is a gap between her sentences, which she seems to have only so she can have a sip of her drink.

"Guess that depends on your definition of using... I have had the app for a while, but don't connect with people very often."

"Right. Yeah. this was my first time using it."

"Yes, you said. When you first sat down."

I nod. And finish my drink.

"Do you want another? Or...?" she pauses and looks at me.

I dread what I think she is suggesting as the *or*. I am not sure how we are so far apart on understanding what my answer will be to her unfinished question. "I'd like another."

She blinks. "Oh. Okay. I will be right back." And she pushes back her chair, picks up our two empties and walks determinedly to the bar. The place is busier now. Very busy for 9 p.m. on a Thursday. Clearly too busy for the bartender to leave her post and traipse drinks to a table on the far side of the room, even for what must be $20 tips.

I find it odd that it is so busy. People should be home, watching television, getting ready for the last day of work for the week, and looking forward to their weekends, making plans to do fun things with loved ones.

Violet is waiting behind someone for our drinks. She is leaning against the bar, looking toward me. I don't let my eyes pause on her. I don't want her to think I am looking at her because I am certain she will take that the wrong way. She will be thinking I am watching her in the way I think she is watching me. But, really, what I am doing is contemplating how to extricate myself from this date, after she has plied me with drinks and is ready to take me home with her. Because I am ready to drink more, and take myself home, later, to my own lonely apartment.

I turn in my seat and look across the room. The place is dimly lit, romantically lit, perhaps, though this romantic ambience isn't reaching me. The dimness just makes the place feel seedy. But maybe that's just me. Perhaps there are couples here on a first date — with, hopefully, a better match than Violet and I — and old couples who want a change of scenery, and groups of women who

just want to get away from their daily lives — their possibly closeted daily lives — who all find this dimness pleasant.

And my eyes find Glen.

She and Sierra are sitting along the side wall, almost directly
behind me. Sierra is mostly blocked from my view by an inter-
vening table of two who are sitting close together, but Glen is
sitting in my direct line of sight, and is turned, facing me.

I literally feel my heart skip a beat. And blood rushes in my
ears.

She is too far away, and the lighting is too dim for me to see her
face clearly. But I know I make eye contact with her. I feel this
contact in a line that runs from my navel to my crotch. A sparking
jolt.

And then Violet sets a Sling in front of me and drops herself
back into her own chair and I have to turn away from this invisible
eye contact and return to face Violet.

"Do you see someone you know?" she asks as she peers past
me, into the dim.

"Oh, I was just checking how busy it got around us, while we
talked here."

"Yeah, I guess you don't know too many people here, huh, you
just got here in the summer, right? Didn't you tell me that? Yeah,
June I think you said. Though that has been several months, so
maybe you made a lot of friends here already. Or friends at university — I know that students typically go to campus pubs, but as
you're queer, maybe some classmates are also queer and come here
too..."

She continues talking while I feel Glen's eyes on my back.

Violet chatters on, if it was hard, before, to pay attention to
what she was saying, the rushing inside my ears and the awareness
of Glen's gaze warming my skin has removed all my ability to
absorb a word Violet speaks.

The urge to get away from the inane chattering, away from this
woman, and to think — to imagine, quietly, being somewhere else

with... someone else — causes me to push my chair back, quickly, suddenly. And I am on my feet before I realize what I am doing.

The chatter stops and Violet looks up at me, puzzled.

I look down at her and, for one short moment, almost tell her I have had enough, and that I must leave. But I don't. I gesture politely to the restroom. "Sorry... I have to run to the little girl's room. Back in a minute."

In the bathroom I stare at myself in the mirror above the sink. I splash cool water on my cheeks, gathering the courage to walk back out there and... just tell Violet I have to go home now. Just a short and sweet 'gotta go', and a quick walk back to the subway... well, I can try that, I guess. I am not confident that approach will work.

When I turn to exit and head back to the expected long and painful conversation waiting for me at the table, Glen steps through the bathroom doorway.

"Everything okay?" she asks with a smile.

Heart in throat, I meet her eyes. "Ummm. I think it's too complicated for me, tonight." I step toward her. I don't have the courage to kiss her, but the urge to lean forward and do so almost moves me forward the one more step I would need.

Her lips quirk. Does she lean to step toward me, or is that my imagination. My eyes rest on her lips. I will move forward. I will feel her mouth on mine.

Violet appears in the doorway then. "There you are." Her four and a half foot self pushes between Glen and I, from the side, and she sticks out her hand to Glen. "I'm Violet. Liz and I are getting to know one another."

Glen looks at Violet's hand and takes it, but her eyes return to me, "Delighted."

Violet's smile dims just a bit and she releases Glen's hand.

I turn to Violet. I don't have to force the regret into my voice, but I will not think about what it is, precisely, I am regretting at this moment. "Violet. I think I have to head out. I am tired, and the drinks have made me... well... tipsy. I don't think I can have

more and I don't want to spoil the rest of the evening. I am...
preoccupied. I hope you understand."

Glen slips out of the bathroom. Violet stares at me.

"Oh. Is that the reason?" she snaps, sarcasm almost visible.
"And I paid for your drinks, spent my whole evening letting you
get to know me, getting to know you..." Her eyes glisten, but I am
very sure she isn't on the edge of tears.

"Yeah. I am sorry. Sorry..." I also exit the bathroom and walk
straight through the bar and out the doors to the street, without
waiting for Violet to say anything else, without looking for Glen,
or Sierra. I just need to get outside where the fresh air will clear my
head.

IT'S ALL FUN AND GAMES UNTIL YOU FIND YOU'VE RUBBED YOUR SLEEVE IN SOMETHING STRANGE

"I THOUGHT you might want to meet closer to the municipal truck depot," Glen sets a Starbucks coffee in front of me and slides into the bench seat beside me, "closer to 5 p.m. though," she glances at her watch and gives me an exaggerated nod, "yup, we're too early..."

"Not funny." I smile at her, shoulder-bumping her gently.

"It looked pretty funny last night." She grins in response. "Anyway, how did it go, really? Did you two leave together? Did you end up having the hanky panky?" She hides her grin behind the coffee cup she is holding to her mouth as she widens her eyes and bats her lashes at me.

I can't help but laugh out loud. "Glen, no." I shake my head. "It wasn't really my... kind of date. Datee? Anyway, Violet is not really my type." I am as polite as I can be. Violet is way beyond not my type to being pretty much the antithesis of the type of woman I would ever date. But I don't really need to say that type of thing out loud.

"So, you and Sierra didn't see Violet after I left?" I look at Glen closely.

"Yeah. I did. I watched you leave, actually... I was just teasing you a bit... at least about the hanky panky..." She smiles, "Maybe app dating is not for you, huh, or maybe you need someone to help you sift through the potentials, not sure how you ended up on a date with Violet... she seems pretty, well, different from who I would imagine you hooking up with."

Glen raises an eyebrow and takes a sip from her cup as she thinks it over, "That might be a good idea... have someone else pick your dates... or, you could just come out with me," she pauses, my heart feels like it pauses with her, for a moment, "and meet people in a more traditional way. At a bar, you know..." She grins wider and winks at me.

I blush and look away, my cheeks feeling hot as I realize just how much I was imagining (hoping, dreaming?) going out with her, just her and me, together. I take a deep breath before answering, "Yeah, been there, done that... didn't work out so good... hah..." At the puzzled look on Glen's face I add, "Oh, yeah, I forgot you don't know the story... it's a long one, but, basically, that's how I met Toni..."

Glen laughs softly and nods her head in understanding, "I get it. Yeah, I can definitely relate to that." She smiles and takes another sip of her drink before continuing, "Trust me, after my messy breakup, the very last thing I wanted was to meet someone at the first bar I go to after arriving on my holiday. I think I thought it was just going to be some drinking and dancing, and, maybe, a drunken hookup with some Canadian chick. Melanie and I were together for years — I thought I might just as well have some fun, be on a rebound in a foreign country. By the end with Mel, it was pretty tough."

She looks thoughtful and is looking down at her hands, still holding her coffee firmly. "We used to have a lot of fun going out, dancing, meeting people. But, we moved to a small town in East Anglia and the closet doors banged shut behind us. We weren't out anymore and the arguments started. All the pressure of hiding who we are, and the people at the pub asking where our boyfriends were — it was so suffocating."

I nod. "So you came to Canada for... a break? A change of scenery? To start fresh maybe?"

A hint of sadness crosses Glen's face as she looks back up at me. "Exactly. It was just shite there. Everything reminded me that I can't be queer there, and it was my job, our jobs — our safety even — on the line, so we didn't have a choice but to stay closeted and... well... I got so frustrated with the whole thing, maybe even the whole country by the end, and here I am. I came here, to Canada for peace and quiet and space to be queer and to sort my head out."

I hadn't realized she was so fresh from a breakup, that Canada was her rebound. "How long were you and... Melanie?... together?"

"Five years. I met her at a club in London and we hit it off... but, anyway, that's the past. The closet living killed our relationship. Whatever... this chat is about you, not me, we have to find you better matches than that app came up with." Her gaze flicks to mine briefly before returning to her now empty coffee.

Is it my imagination, or do I hear something more lingering in her tone?

But before I can think about it any further, Glen continues, "Anyway, if you want company going out, keep me in mind. Could be cathartic for us both to make new memories, unrelated to our pasts. Bar involved or not."

There is some meaning here, in her offer. Her eyes hold mine for a moment, and then for another moment. There is a look in them I'm afraid to interpret.

I don't even think about Sierra.

"Want another coffee?" Glen pops out of her seat and is heading to the counter before I have a chance to respond.

I find myself watching Glen's figure move across the room. A feeling of warmth spreads through my chest. I can hear her accent as she orders from the barista and both she and the barista laugh. Glen's laugh makes my heart flutter for a second.

"What the hell are you doing, Liz." I mutter quietly, out loud, to myself.

Liking it Spicy

SUNDAY AFTERNOON I am at Sierra's place. Glen had called me just before I headed out to work my night shift last evening and invited me for dinner. I went home after work and managed to get a few hours sleep, but some weird and more than likely inappropriate excitement churning in my belly woke me earlier than was ideal after working a 12 hour night shift.

I get off the subway a stop early to pick up a bottle of Tanqueray gin that Glen had mentioned she liked. I walk the rest of the way to Sierra's and stand in the building's foyer looking at the buzzers.

A tinny voice squawks from the speaker below the buzzers, startling me "No soliciting," it pauses, "unless you're a solicitor."

Even through the tinny, oddly loud buzzer speaker, I recognize the voice. The accent possibly, but I think it is the voice itself that I can still hear in my head as the door makes a long buzzing noise.

Sierra opens the apartment door when I knock. I force myself to ignore the sinking in my belly that it's not Glen. I knew Sierra would be here, of course, and I would not have turned down this invitation for any reason I can think of, including Sierra being here, but the thought of hours of conversation that will be geared to include Sierra feels like a weight pressing on my chest. She takes the bottle of gin from my hand and steps back to let me in.

"Glen!" Sierra shouts as she swings the door closed behind me, "Liz brought that horrible gin you drink."

Glen, who is just in the kitchen on the far side of the same room, stirring something in a pot, could probably hear Sierra just fine without the shouting, glances over at us, "That horrible stuff, excellent. I love that horrible gin."

Sierra plops the bottle on the island and steps up to Glen and kisses her, wet and sloppy and too long for when you have company standing just on the other side of the kitchen island, watching you.

When Sierra finally pulls her face off Glen's, Glen steps to the side and pulls open the fridge door. She takes out a can of beer and a large bottle of tonic.

Sierra takes the beer from her. "I'll leave that paint remover to you gals."

Glen gets two glasses from the cupboard beside the stove and places them on the island in front of me. She doesn't make eye contact with me as she returns to face the pot on the stove. Sierra passes me, heading to the couch with the can of beer.

"Do you have ice?" I ask her as I step into the kitchen. Sierra grunts in what I take as a yes. I slide open the freezer drawer and there is an open bag of ice and a frozen pizza in there. Nothing else.

I sense Glen move closer. She is looking into the freezer drawer with me. "Sierra likes those frozen pizzas. I like Pizza Pizza delivery better. Well, my absolute favorite is the Pizza Pizza by the slice, at that place across from Petals. There is something, delicious, about luke warm pizza at 3 a.m. when you've just had a great evening hanging out and dancing."

She brushes against me and grabs a handful of ice from the bag. She steps to the island and drops the ice into one glass, turns back, brushes against me again, and takes a second handful. I slide the freezer drawer closed and stand beside her at the island, my hip touching hers as she opens the Tanqueray bottle and fills the glasses to just about halfway.

"Bring me a beer when you come over." Sierra is still sitting on the couch. The TV is on, but muted. Sports. Football, by the looks of it. Well, football here, in Canada, not football as Glen would know it.

Glen pours a splash of tonic into one of the glasses and tilts the bottle toward the other glass. She looks at me, making eye contact for the first time since I arrived.

I just look at her for a second. Then a second more. Then I nod and she tips the tonic bottle to splash some into the second glass. She sets the bottle down and picks up one of the glasses and holds it out to me until I take it. Then she picks up her own glass. She has not broken eye contact, I have not broken eye contact. The static buzzing in my ears feels electric.

She clinks her glass against mine, "To terrible... gin..." Her lips touch the edge of her glass. I break eye contact and watch her lips as she takes a sip.

"Uh, beer? Hello. What the hell is taking you guys so long, it's just gin and tonic, not that complicated to mix."

And Glen sets her glass down and I step backward out of the kitchen space and Glen opens the fridge again and gets a can of beer. And I take a seat in the Queen Anne chair which is turned a bit to face the television. Glen joins Sierra on the couch, handing her the beer before sitting herself. Sierra puts her arm around Glen and nods at the TV. "This is football. Glen doesn't agree," she tightens her arm around Glen's shoulder, tugging her closer, "right, my little Brit?"

* * *

Glen and I finish our gin about the same time as Sierra finishes her beer, and when Glen stands to get refills for us, Sierra pops up with her, "I'm starved, that chili done yet?"

The table has already been set, so Sierra takes the seat I was in the night I stayed here. I am surprised to think that was already more than a week ago. It feels like it was just the night before last. I follow Glen to the kitchen where she ladles chili into bowls. I take two bowls to the table and set one in front of Sierra.

I pass the seat that Glen had sat in the other night and take the last seat with a place setting. My back is to the living room, and the TV but, most importantly, I am directly facing Glen and not Sierra, who is already spooning chili into her mouth. I hear her slurping.

"This is great," Sierra speaks with her mouth full of chili.

"Thanks." Glen is buttering some bread from a basket on the table. "Liz?" she holds the piece of bread out toward me. I take it, from the underside, and let my fingers touch the back of her hand for a second too long.

She butters a second piece and hands it to Sierra, who immediately dunks it into her chili bowl.

The chili is mild. And tomato-y.

"Glen's a great cook. She cooks at home, in England, you know," Sierra talks around the bread she is chewing. "First time she made chili for me it was so hot it burned my stomach for hours. She makes it much better now."

I nod. And continue eating the chili, thinking that it would be much better, if it were hotter.

"I toned it down, quite a lot, for Sierra." Glen looks directly at me. "I do prefer mine spicy. The more spicy the better. Hot..."

"Hon, can you get me a beer," Sierra interrupts.

Glen does so. And returns with two more gins too.

Only Rocks to Offer

A BUZZING BLAT STARTLES ME. I jolt awake, unware that I had fallen asleep, my Margaret Atwood novel closed on my lap. The blat repeats. It must be my doorbell. I have never heard it ring... blat... before. I glance at the clock as I get out of the recliner: 3:30. I have only been home an hour, so my nap couldn't have been for long. I am very groggy though, so it must have been a much-needed nap.

I am halfway up the stairs when the blat comes again. I wonder who would be so persistent. I don't have any neighbors upstairs yet, the previous family moved out the first of November, and the new ones don't move in until December. And I can't imagine that a delivery person would keep buzzing, or that I have anything being delivered. It is too early for Christmas gifts and I haven't shopped online in ages. Toni did, a lot, so maybe she forgot to update the shipping address in her online account and it ended up here. I hope this is not the case because I don't want to call her to come get it, and I don't want to talk to her when she comes to get it. I don't really want whatever it is and, as I open the door, I decide I will refuse delivery. Not my problem.

Glen stands at my door.

A shiver runs down my spine.

I stare at her, my words caught in my own mouth.

"Hi," she greets me, her voice soft and her accent thick. She is still standing there — her rucksack beside her leaning against the wall — several seconds later when I finally find some words.

"Ummm. Hi. Uh..." my eyes flit to the empty parking spaces, uncertain, "how'd you get here? Uh. I didn't know you knew where I lived, actually." Her eyes hold me captive, then I realize she is still standing there. "Oh, come in, sorry, I was just reading, well, I thought I was reading, turns out I was napping. And now I am making about the same amount of sense as if I were still napping, actually..."

Glen smiles, and lifts the rucksack by the hand strap at the top. Inside, I feel like I am squirming.

We descend the stairs together. My heart beats in sync with our steps. "Grand tour: there is the bathroom," I gesture toward the door directly at the bottom of the stairs. We turn left through a doorless frame, "and here is the 250 square foot living and dining lounge." I wave my arm to demonstrate. Pointing to the doorway, also doorless, that leads to the kitchen, I add, "That is the kitchen, it has just about enough space to turn around."

I deliberately avoid pointing to the room on the left. That room, with its open door, clearly displays the unmade bed.

"Do you want something to drink? I have, ummm, water. And gin. And maybe some vodka, but maybe not, I don't drink vodka much." I bite my tongue to stop myself from babbling. I know I don't have any vodka. I have no idea why I am rambling on.

Glen's choice is, unsurprisingly — and fortunately — gin. I instruct her to have a seat while I go scrounge for something to mix with the gin. When I return to the living room, she is rifling through my Atwood book. I hand her a drink and sit on the couch beside her, "I don't have any mix, hope you like gin on the rocks?"

She closes the book and sets it on the coffee table, well, cardboard boxes with a strip of fabric over them which I call a coffee table, "Never could get into Atwood's writing. Too, well, esoteric. In fact, I bet she's esoteric enough that she actually uses the word esoteric in her writings!" Glen frowns at the book on the coffee table. "Do you have that in digital? We could word search."

I don't agree with Glen's assessment of Atwood's work, but I don't feel like getting into a discussion on the importance of embedding feminist approaches into fiction. "I don't read much in digital, actually. But I think we could find it online? If you're that keen?"

She drinks half the drink and leans back against the cushions. "Fuck."

I drink half my drink and set it carefully beside the Atwood book. "What's up? Where is Sierra? Why are you here?" She meets my gaze and finishes her drink. "I have other questions to ask too, but let's just start with these three, okay?"

"Okay. three questions... what's up? I left Sierra's. Oh, wait, that answers all three. Shouldn't I get a prize?" She holds up the glass of ice.

Wetter Things

"So, what's the story?" We have finished a second gin on ice and Glen does not want a third. I bring her one anyway and set it on the makeshift coffee table.

We are still sitting on the couch. Glen speaks quietly, "She just drinks too much. And she's not a nice drunk. "

"Oh." This is not a surprise. Of course I have seen Sierra drinking before. She's a big girl and a fast drinker, and if I had to pick a single adjective to describe her after a couple drinks, it would be belligerent. And I am not certain she even needs the drinks to be in that state.

"Anyway, I am not in Canada to settle down. I came to explore, and I wasn't doing that, with Sierra."

My chest tightens. "So, you're, what... heading out for greener pastures?"

"Wetter ones anyway, there is a hostel in Niagara Falls, I don't think I can come all this way and not at least see that. I think I'll go there for a night, and then carry on west, so, maybe greener too, if I make it to the prairies, huh."

"Dunno, Never been." I speak into my glass.

She leans forward, beside me on the couch — I assume to pick up her drink.

But she turns toward me and takes the glass from my hand. She finishes the remaining liquid and sets it beside hers on the coffee table. She runs her fingers up my arm. My skin prickles.

"I've wanted to do this since I first laid eyes on you at Petals," she leans toward me and kisses me. Her lips are full, and soft and her mouth is warm and tastes like gin.

She leans into me, pressing me sideways on the couch, until she is lying half on top of me, half beside me. Her mouth doesn't leave mine.

Her tongue plays with mine. I run mine along her bottom lip, against her teeth. Her hand passes along my ribs, down to my waist, then back up under my shirt. Her hand brushes heavily, with pressure, up and over my breast. Her palm passes over my nipple, back, over, back, lightly, brushing. Her mouth, warm and wet and pressing. Her tongue, playing, teasing. I feel the heat and damp in my crotch. I think it started when I saw her standing outside my door, with her rucksack, but now it is all I am aware of. That ache in my groin, the heat, the wet, her mouth, her tongue, pressing, insisting. Her soft dry hand brushing...

I slide my free hand along her body, from where it can reach, at her hip, up to her back. I can't feel her skin except at her lower back where I can get my hand under her shirt. But the shirt won't slide up, the front of it is pinned between our bodies and the fabric is stiff. I try to shift, to move out from under her, so she will be under me, and I can access her skin and kiss her and touch her wet and warm...

The door buzzer blats.

The noise literally jolts Glen up. She slides off the edge of the couch, onto her knees. She is facing me, flushed. I sit up, sideways on the couch. And swing my legs over. My lips miss hers and I lean to kiss her again. To hell with the door.

"What was that?" she moves back from me and gets to her feet.

The blat comes again. This time it doesn't stop for several seconds. "Someone is holding in the doorbell," I tug my shirt back into place.

"That's Sierra," Glen takes my hand, "I don't think you should let her in."

It had to be Sierra. The warmth in my core fades. I feel clammy. I look through the open bedroom door to see if I can see a car in the parking space, but I can't see one. She could have parked in the driveway, or not pulled all the way into the parking spot. I can't see beyond the first foot out the window from here, but if it is Sierra, and it has to be Sierra, because the odds of it being anyone else are, well, astronomical — my doorbell never rings, so it ringing twice in the same afternoon for unconnected events is not realistic — she wouldn't know where to park, or that she could park here at all. So she could be parked out front on the street, or in the parking lot of the Jamaican patty shop...

Glen and I stand there, holding hands for another minute when I hear a fast rapping on the window in the bedroom.

"This is like some horror movie. I always wondered why the women just stand frozen and wait to be murdered," I step toward the bedroom. I will look out the window and see. If it is Sierra, and she is peering in the window, I will crank it open and let her know that I am not going to let her in.

Glen squeezes my hand. "I don't think you should let her see you. She will go away, if she thinks you're not here."

"Will she though? I don't know Sierra super well, but I would not be surprised if she sits out there until she sees me come or go." I look at Glen, "But how would she even know you're here? How did you know where I lived? Sierra doesn't know, so she couldn't have told you..."

"No. I called Jackie."

"Jackie?" The name is out of place in this context. I can't think of who Glen could be referring to. It would make no sense to be the only Jackie I know of.

"Sierra's ex. She knew your address." Glen pauses, "She was here before, with Toni."

"Oh. My. God. Are you serious?" My mind starts spinning, "Sierra's ex, Jackie, who, coincidentally, Toni left me for, is now giving my address out to anyone who asks?" I pointedly ignore the revelation that Jackie had been here — that Toni had brought her here — and that it seems I might be the only person who did not know this.

Not that I mind Glen having my address.

But I definitely would prefer that Sierra did not.

And I would prefer it if the woman Toni left me for would stop giving out my address. The flush that fills my cheeks is no longer related to Glen's touch.

I step into the bedroom and walk close enough to the window so I can see feet outside, and, on my tiptoes, the front end of a car in the parking spot.

"I can't imagine she would have given Sierra your address," Glen speaks from the doorway behind me. "I can't imagine Sierra would have contacted her. At least not until she was loaded, and then she wouldn't have made it all the way out here..."

"No. It's not Sierra."

I pivot and head up the stairs. I am turning the knob to open the door when there is another doorbell blat, which cuts off immediately as I swing the door open.

Toni is standing there.

"Hi," she says.

"Toni. What the fuck."

"Can I come in?"

"No."

She looks puzzled. "I know Glen is here."

"And?"

"She called Jackie's. She was looking for how to find our place. Your place," she corrects herself quickly.

"And?"

"Are you okay?" She reaches toward me.

Unable to determine if she is trying to open the door farther and let herself in, or to embrace me, I stiffen. "Toni. Why are you here?"

"I was worried about you." She tries to peer past me, "Is she here? This isn't good, Liz, she's bad news."

"Who? Sierra?" I am confused.

"No, Glen. She will move in and live off you until she is done with you, and then she'll move on to her next destination, her next 'girlfriend.'"

I wonder if Toni understands irony.

"Toni. What do you want?"

"I just wanted to make sure you're okay. I don't want you to be rebounding into something..."

"Trouble in paradise?" Glen presses against me from behind, her chin resting on my shoulder as we look out the door at Toni. Glen cups my butt near the center, with both hands, squeezing gently. "Possibly Jackie isn't all she was cracked up to be?"

Toni glares at Glen.

"Liz. What are you doing?" Toni asks me without taking her eyes off Glen.

I wonder what Glen knows about Toni. Or about Jackie. Or how close she was to Jackie to be able to call her to find out my address. And why would Jackie give Glen my address, and why would Jackie then tell Toni that she gave Glen my address.

"None of this makes sense."

A long awkward silence drags out in the stairwell, with Toni standing just outside, Glen standing just behind me, and me wondering what I am supposed to do now — short of telling Toni to go away, and sitting Glen down to demand some straight answers.

Though, feeling the heat from Glen's body seeping into me as she leans against me from behind, I know for certain that telling Toni to go away won't lead me to the couch and a conversation with Glen. Our next step will involve a shower and a bed and hours of exploration.

Glen's lips brush against the side of my neck, just below my ear. Then she steps backward down the stairs, "You know. I saw a

Coffee Time by the subway stop. How about I go get us some coffees. Give you a bit of time to discuss... whatever..."

I am relieved at her offered solution, "That would be great, actually. I could use a coffee, even if..." I stop speaking, I don't know what the end of my statement could be... *even if it I don't know why you are here with me, Glen, how you got here, why Toni is here, why Toni left in the first place, who the hell is this Jackie that everyone but me seems to have some intimate knowledge of, and, is Sierra gonna be the next person to show up at the door.*

"That's all that's missing," I mutter as I also head downstairs. Toni follows.

"What's missing?" Toni asks behind me. Glen waits for us to pass her at the bottom of the stairs before heading up the stairs herself.

"Oh, was just talking to myself, out loud I guess. Just wondering who's gonna show up here next, and if Glen needs to get a box of coffee just in case."

* * *

Toni waits for the thunk of the apartment door to indicate that Glen has indeed left. "I told you I loved you. I didn't want to leave. That was your choice." Toni's eyes move from spot to spot in the room, as if she is checking to see what has changed in the weeks she has been gone.

"Umm. that's not really how I remember it went." I am sitting in the recliner, Toni on the solitary hardback kitchen chair, facing me.

Her eyes land on the two glasses on the coffee table, "Mid afternoon, Liz?"

"Toni, what the hell are you doing here? And, anyway, it's nearly evening. And, night, elsewhere." I wonder why I am defending myself.

"Like in England?" Toni shakes her head, "Anyway, I'm not

here to talk about your drinking habits. Glen called Jackie this morning, early, like before work early, to get your address."

"That isn't explaining why you are here."

She leans forward in the chair, "Liz, why are you so being so difficult. I told you. I still love you."

"Okay, so let me see if I understand. You starting fucking Jackie before Thanksgiving, while Jackie was still fucking Sierra. Then Jackie dumps Sierra and Sierra meets Glen and then you tell me you met Jackie — which was a lie, of course, wasn't it Toni? — and that you wanted a job with her so were going to go away for a weekend of sex-capades, and then come back to me like I'm the good little wife paying the bills and keeping house?"

"That's not fair."

"Not fair? What the fuck? You know what's not fair? Me, working 20 hours a week at a fucking mall in Thornhill, working 24 hours on weekend overnights, spending about 20 hours a week on fucking public transit, and still having to complete a graduate degree program that expects I work less than 12 hours a week total. I am tired, Toni. So fucking tired." I snatch one of the glasses off the coffee table and take it with me into the kitchen, where I don't even bother dumping the melted ice before refilling it.

I finish it and leave the glass on the counter.

When I return to the living room, Toni hasn't moved.

"It was only attraction Liz. I was attracted to Jackie."

"Was? What happened, she got what she wanted, a little bit of that French-loving, and is done with you?"

"C'mon, you know I don't connect sex to love that same way. I don't love Jackie. It was just sex. I do love you."

"Trouble is, Toni, I do. I do connect it. I can't lie here in bed and think about my girlfriend fucking someone else and then coming home to me with her scent on your lips."

Even discussing it makes my eyes prick. I close them so they won't cry.

"I would never do that..."

"Never mind Toni. Is this why you're here? To tell me that you want to come back? To ask if I'm willing to be number one harem girl? — that you love me long time?"

"Not really. Or not exactly... I am here because of Glen. I don't want to see you hurt."

I suddenly realize that Toni is speaking what she thinks is the truth. She thinks she loves me and that her sexual trysts are innocent and that her interest in warning me about Glen is for my own well-being. I flop back into the recliner.

"She came here and immediately moved in with Sierra, stays rent free and doesn't pay for anything, not groceries, not booze, not bus fare. She has some mystery job in England, which she never talks about, and was planning to return to it early November, then something changes and it's now not until December, apparently."

A spark of happiness jars me when Toni mentions Glen being here until December. I hadn't realized it, but her departure date being so close was hanging over my head. Glen must have changed her flight; she had mentioned that she was considering doing that, but had wanted to see how much she was enjoying her travels, and how much traveling she got in first. She had learned that visiting Canada was not quite on the same scale as visiting a European country.

I know this is not Toni's intended result, but it makes me smile.

"Why are you smiling?"

"Toni. I don't know what you want me to say. Or what you expect me to do. We are finished. I am not taking you back."

At this, Toni puts her face in her hands and I can see her shaking. She is crying.

I don't offer any comfort. I don't think I can. I don't think I want to. The part of me that might have had comfort to give is exhausted. Tired and exhausted and emotionally drained, and I don't want to. I wish I had brought a drink back in with me, to sip this time, so I wouldn't be sitting here, feeling awkward and callous but not willing to do anything about it.

I close my eyes and just sit still. I don't doze off, but I can feel the spinny tiredness behind my eyes. A few minutes pass and I hear Toni let herself out.

I have to get out of the recliner some time later to answer yet another doorbell blat. The door's automatic locking is actually appreciated — under my usual visitors' schedule anyway — because then I never have to wonder as I drop into bed mid-morning after getting home from my night shift if I remembered to lock it.

This thought leads to a new thought and I realize I need to find a place to stash a spare, just in case I lock myself out. The surge of loneliness this thought causes nearly chokes me.

This time when I open the door, it is Glen standing there, with three large coffees in a cardboard tray.

"Toni's gone already?"

"Yeah," I take the tray from her and we descend the stairs, "She has said what she felt she needed to say. And I told her I had to get ready for work." I set the tray of coffees on the coffee table and look at the clock. "And, unfortunately, I didn't make that part up. I have to get out of here soon, or I'll be late." I rub my face with my hands, so drained I just want to fold into a ball on the couch and sleep for a month. "Do you want to stay here tonight? Or do you have a place lined up...?"

She takes my hands into hers and looks at me closely. "Are you okay?"

I want to lean in and kiss her and tug her shirt over her head and unclip her bra and take her hard dark nipple into my mouth and...

I smile, "Yes. Just tired. And perverted. And late for work..." I pick up one of the coffees and pop the lid off.

"They're all black." Glen picks up the brown paper bag from the fourth cup hole in the cardboard tray that must hold the creamers and sugars. "I didn't know what Toni took in her coffee."

The coffee is just warm so I drink half of it in one go.

She sips her coffee, without taking the lid off. She darts her tongue out, as if she is looking for the drinking hole. I watch her lips. I imagine I can still feel them against my own. Her tongue...

"Okay. Glen. You gotta stop looking at me, or drinking, or whatever it is you're doing, or I gotta go have a cold shower." I walk backward toward the bathroom with the paper coffee cup in hand, "Oh, okay. AND I will have to go have a cold shower. I can't be late. I have to shower. I would love to have you join me. But, I can't be late for work. So. You have to stay out here. Sit. Read a book. Watch TV..."

She winks at me, "I can do that. I will sit here quietly and just think lewd thoughts about you."

I consider locking the bathroom door, my thoughts are equally lewd and I don't know that I would wait in her living room while she showered in an adjacent room.

I do not lock the door. And, as I hop into the shower, I wonder if I hope she'll slip in with me.

She does not and, when I come back to the living room, she has cleared away the coffee tray and its contents, and the gin glass, and is sitting in the recliner with my Atwood book in her hands. She looks up at me as I walk into the bedroom to get dressed. I am wrapped in a large towel.

"I am not getting out of this chair," she calls after me as I root through the closet to find a clean uniform shirt.

"That's a good plan," I call back.

When I am dressed, I return to the living room. She watches me. "Oh, 'er, I do like a girl in uniform."

I laugh. "Officer Liz, at your service."

Glen puts the legs of the recliner down.

"Oh. NO. Don't come here. I am going. Now." I lift my jacket off the coat rack by the stairs and back up them, "I hope you stay. I should be home around 9. The door self-locks so, if you go out, take a key." I point to the key hook next to the coat rack. And I leave.

Part 3: Looking for Home

I CRAWL OUT OF BED.

Glen rolls to face me, "So early?"

"Yeah, today I have morning classes, then work at the mall. I should be home by 7 though, it won't be a late day."

"7? that's a long day!" She pats the bed beside her, "Why not just play hooky and come back here."

"Hah. I did that yesterday, remember? Can't afford to do it again. Gotta pay the rent on this mansion."

She pouts, exaggerating this by pushing out her bottom lip and blinking her eyes rapidly, "It's only one day. One more day I mean... I don't have any plans today."

I don't mention that she doesn't have any plans, any day. Because I haven't minded. She is home when I get here and we spend most of our time in bed. I don't think she has gone out, anywhere, since she got here. Well, other than to the coffee shop near the subway.

"As much as I want to..." I don't finish my sentence as I head for the shower.

I just finish putting a drop of shampoo into my very short hair and am running my fingers through it when the shower curtain is pulled back and Glen steps into the shower with me, "I will help, that will save you some time this morning."

She steps close to me and puts her hands under the water. She picks up the bar soap from the soap tray and rolls it in her hands until they are soapy, then she drops the soap and I feel it bump against the side of my foot as it slides to the drain. She puts her hands on each side of my waist, just above my hips. She slides her hands upward and around to my lower back, then down, one hand running along each butt cheek to where they turn into my legs. She tugs — squeezes — very lightly at the join.

Her breasts are pressing into me. Her mouth captures my nipple. She bites it, gently. The current runs straight down to my navel — lower. The water sprays down on my head and shampoo suds roll down my neck, my face, my chest. I pull her head up with my left hand while I steady myself against the wall with my right.

Her mouth meets mine, her tongue slides in, familiar now, tasting of morning and a hint of our sex from last night. She turns so there is space between us, on the curtained side of the tub, still with her mouth pressing into mine and her tongue brushing along my teeth and she slides her right hand along the outside of my hip to my bush. Her fingers cup, her fingertips just brushing the very front of my fold.

Her arm is bent awkwardly. I don't let her mouth go. And her fingers slide in, and over my clit. Her fingers grip me, one on either side, slick with water and with my own wetness. She moves them quickly, pressing firmly upward, cupping my cunt with the rest of her fingers, but keeping my clit trapped between two. She moves them rhythmically, firmly, quickly, her tongue and her mouth sucking and pressing and rubbing.

And I come with a grunt against her lips. "Fuck."

"Later. You have to get to work, remember?" She steps back from me and yanks the curtain open at the far end of the tub, "Now, go, I don't want to run out of hot water."

* * *

"That sounds like a great plan, actually."

Glen and I are sitting at the coffee shop near the subway. I have to get to campus for a late morning class, then will go right from there to work. We walked here for coffee, mainly so we would get out of bed.

"Yeah, I think I will be disappointed if I don't get to see Niagara Falls. And, you're sure you won't be able to go with me, maybe on a different day?"

"I don't think so. I have so much work to do for school, I have been, uh, slacking for the last couple weeks... not sure why..."

She kicks me gently under the table. "Really. Wonder why that is?"

I ignore her lewd grin. "We could go during the university Christmas break though, that's only a couple weeks out. I will have so much extra time when I don't have to be commuting half the day — I can go directly to work and home..."

Glen looks at me directly. "Sweetie. I won't be here at Christmas break."

I stop talking.

"I have to go home the week after next."

"But, can't you change your flight? Now that..."

"I did, already, but the flight isn't why I have to go home. I have to get back to work, the pub's busy at Christmas and I can't be a lady of leisure forever. I've already been gone longer than I had thought, when I started out."

"But you haven't seen Canada..." I sound lame even to myself.

"That's why I am going to Niagara Falls this weekend. You'll be working Saturday night, sleeping on Sunday..."

"And working on my research project with Cherry on Sunday afternoon..." I finish her explanation for her. She is correct. It is the best time for her to be going to Niagara Falls. But I don't add that part, or indicate that I am actually feeling a bit relieved that I will have that time to work on my project without missing her as she sits alone at the apartment.

But the weight of realization that she is returning to England, sooner rather than later, creates a sick knot in my stomach. I stare at my coffee. It is not a surprise, logically I knew she was going to have to go back to England, I just hadn't let myself think about that.

And I thought maybe, just maybe, she could stay longer, with me.

"You can stay with me. You don't have to go home because you don't have a place." I still sound lame, and whiny even.

"I know Liz, I know I am welcome, but at some point I will have to start contributing, and I can't work here, I only have a tourist visa, and, anyway, the pub really does need me for the Christmas holidays..."

I look up at the sound of a 'but' in her voice.

"A week or two after New Year's though, the pub gets pretty quiet, for a couple months anyway, there are no events in January at all, and February is just Valentines... after that it picks up again, heading into spring and we have boules tourneys and all."

"So you could, what? Come back here after Christmas?" The excitement, the relief, actually makes my voice crack.

"Possibly." She smiles and puts her hand on top of mine on top of the table, "Or you might like England? Our winters are way nicer than I understand they are here..."

I let the idea stay in my head for a minute, imagining a winter in a land that didn't get snow, where Glen would be working and I would be lounging around the apartment waiting for her to come home. Or, maybe, waiting for her at work where I could watch her work, and maybe sneak off together to the bathroom on her breaks.

A flutter of excitement rushes within me.

"Think about it," she urges, her thumb tracing small circles on the back of my hand. "I'd love to show you around, introduce you to my world."

I nod, still processing the idea. The prospect of experiencing her world, even temporarily, was appealing. Yet, the practicalities of leaving behind my job — my jobs — and my studies, and my apartment which I wouldn't be able to afford if I wasn't working...

"Are you thinking you'll be staying there. I mean, not coming back to Canada?" I ask, the weight of the decision I will have to make settling on my shoulders.

Glen's gaze remains fixed on mine. "I can see you there. I can see you living there, you would like it," she replies, quietly.

"I don't know how I would... school... ummm..." I hadn't thought this relationship through. I hadn't wanted to. I don't want to. My voice just trails off, I don't even know what I could say next.

Glen nods, "Now's not the time to make that decision... I might only stay there for the holidays and come back, you might just come over for your holidays, or, maybe, you'll like it there and want to stay, in the end. Lots of time to think about it."

I can't pinpoint if the fluttering I feel is panic or excitement. Can I really consider going to England with her? What can I do with my life and responsibilities here?

"As much as I'd love to be with you, I can't just drop everything," I say, slowly. I don't tell her that I am not sure how I could quit everything that I spent all my time and energy on for the past six months. How could I throw away all this exhaustion and effort and just go trailing after Glen to England?

How can I?

Glen nods understandingly, "I know, it's a lot to ask. But maybe you can just think about coming to visit, over the holidays, after exams? Even just for a couple weeks, and we can see how it goes."

The idea is tempting. More than tempting. My mind is already trying to sift through how I could arrange two weeks, or three, and not lose my jobs, or my apartment.

Glen smiles, and squeezes my hand. "But now, sweetie, you have to get your ass to class. We will talk more about it later, when you get home."

A Project

LOVING SAPPHO

SHE HAS a bruise on the inside of her arm that starts just above her elbow and runs upward. I glimpse it as she extends her arm to hand me my drink.

I take the drink, and have a sip while she takes her own seat beside me. I find a place on the cluttered coffee table top to set it. We have our research notes and someone else's thesis printed out and split between us. We downloaded this thesis on observer observations from the university library and Cherry is trying to help me understand what her project is while she is watching me put together some thoughts on my own project — which is, apparently, one of the key activities in her project.

"What's that?" I nod at her bruised arm.

"Just Herbie. It's nothing."

"Cherry! How? That's not nothing."

"We just have that kind of relationship. It's the Italian blood, we get excited and are both... uh... expressive." She starts to take a drink of her own, and must see the look on my face, "Oh! He didn't hit me! If that's what you're thinking! No, I hold my own. We just argued and he shoved me and I shoved him back and lost my balance. Hit that..." she points to a wooden pillar in the apartment's foyer.

"Uh huh. You know we study this stuff, right? In university. You can't have violence in your domestic life. It's not okay."

"It's not violence, it's just passion. He doesn't hit me, or abuse me. It's just we argue and I don't step back from it. I am just extra mad this time. That was my bust of Sappho. I made it myself."

I look over at the pillar, "It looks like a wooden pillar to me."

She laughs. I join her. "Yeah. It was not a bad sculpting, all things considered. I don't do a lot of sculpting, so when Herbie knocked it over... well... I was pretty upset. I mostly just draw, sketch, actually."

She practically jumps off her seat, "Gimme a minute," and she disappears down the hallway to, I imagine, the bedroom. When she returns, she is carrying a sketch book, which she hands to me, "This is from my Sapphic phase."

We make eye contact. Hers are on the darker side of hazel tonight and appear both serious and mischievous.

"Phase. Huh." I flip through her sketches. She has replicated some of the image fragments that remain of Sappho. Some of the pages also have short fragment contents written below the sketches. I am speechless. "This is terrific, Cherry, I didn't know you drew."

"My undergrad is in fine arts, actually. I did my undergrad thesis on Sappho — as you can tell, I was a little obsessed with her."

I finish looking through her sketch book and hand it back to her. Our fingers rest against each other as she takes it. She holds my eyes, and the book.

I let go of it.

She trots it back down the hallway. I return to reviewing my research notes and try to organize them by predominant theme: alcohol being the thickest pile, with family rejection being a close second. I clip sticky notes to each stack of papers, identifying their themed contents.

Cherry returns, sliding smoothly onto the couch beside me

and scooping the stack of papers with the alcohol sticky note onto her lap so she wouldn't sit on them.

Her eyes scan my notes. "Alcohol is a loaded topic," she remarks with a straight face.

I laugh out loud. "I suppose it can be. I guess moderation is always the key. But for some, that line seems to blur pretty easily." My eyes drift back to her bruise.

Cherry follows my gaze and shrugs off my unspoken concern. "Herbie has his stresses just as I do. As we all do. We're not so different underneath it all," she glances at the pillar, "though I do wish I had a photo of it, at least, it really was my favorite piece."

I have a surprising urge to probe further into their relationship. But don't want to make her uncomfortable and, since I can't pinpoint why I would even want to know more, I let the urge go.

To change my headspace as much as the topic, I ask about her art. "Why Sappho? Why sculpting when you mainly sketch?"

Cherry smiles faintly, "It was cathartic to imagine her through my hands. To capture even a glimpse of the woman behind the fragments she left was like bringing a lost poet back to life, if only for myself, and only in plaster."

The afternoon passes quickly and I am surprised when I glance at the wall clock. Glen will be back from her day trip to Niagara Falls before long. Cherry sees me glance at the clock and echoes my thoughts out loud, "Time flies! Herbie will be home soon."

She closes her notebook and helps me pack away my papers.

"I think your project is much easier. You just watch me work, and take notes."

She nods.

"Wish I had thought of your project," I tease, "mine is overwhelming." I am startled by my own honesty.

"You'll get there. You're just expecting it to be done, already, it's a two year program you know. This is only the first semester. What are you planning to do over the summer? You could get a lot of work done then, without classes and the assistantship work to think about."

"I think next summer is so far away right now I can't even guess what my plans might be," is what I say, but I know I could guess, if I wanted to. I could guess that next summer will be just like the past summer, will be just like now... "though, probably I will just work extra overnight shifts, and try to get ahead on some research so the academic year is a bit less hectic next year."

She takes my hand and squeezes my fingers. "You need to work less, you're burning yourself out. Graduate school is supposed to be your full-time job, not a second, or even third job."

I lean in and kiss her.

Her lips are soft and dry and she kisses me back, gently. She doesn't feel surprised.

She doesn't let go of my hand. She pulls me closer and puts her other arm around the small of my back and holds me there. Her mouth is soft and warm and her kiss is gentle and dry and her mouth opens for me and I press into her, my free hand in her hair, holding her head, my fingers tangled in her tangles.

And she pulls her mouth away and I drop my hand from her hair as we hear a key in the lock of the apartment door. We both step back from each other.

Herbie steps into the hallway and kicks off his shoes, "Hey, you must be Liz."

Cherry and I work to steady our breathing as I begin packing my papers into my bag. Her fingers brush mine as she assists. Her eyes showing, something... remorse, lust?

"Liz, I..."

I shake my head subtly. This isn't what I need, what either of us needs right now.

Herbie clatters around in the kitchen while I finish stuffing my things into my bag, then he joins us, a beer in hand. He looks from Cherry to me and back; he seems to have picked up on the tension between us, "Everything alright?"

Cherry smiles at him, "Just digging into the project. It will be interesting, just... a lot of work, and it's hard to figure out what we need to do next." She hasn't stopped looking at me.

Herbie nods, looking at us both, again, then flops on the couch and clicks on the TV. "Looks like you're done, and it's game time, so don't mind me."

Cherry nods, "Sunday football. It's his thing," then softly adds, "Walk you out?"

As we descend the stairs, Cherry stops me on the landing and touches my cheek with a sigh. "This thing between us... I know you can't, I probably can't. But there is something. Something... about you." Her thumb traces my jawline, moving toward my lips. Her eyes rest on my mouth.

I relax into feeling her touch, memorizing it, wondering at the calm in it, and thinking about her lips on mine, before reluctantly stepping back, "Yeah. You're right."

Her hand drops to her side, and she turns and walks back up the stairs.

On a Jet Plane

AND, all of a sudden, the day is here. Glen's departure day. She is returning to England. Her plane leaves in just a few short hours and then... what? Then... what?

The past weeks are a blur. It feels like I just met her, but also like we have been together for ages. She is the bright spot in my overwhelmed life — my insistent, confused, overwhelmed life. Reality seeping in brings the prick of tears to my eyes.

I have been ignoring reality. I knew all along that she would have to return to England. I just wanted to be swept up into the fantasy of forever — I just want to live in that fantasy. Maybe I need to live there...

She's still here, but the bedroom feels cold and empty already. I sit on a pile of folded blankets at the end of the bed, my fingers tracing where Glen's warmth had been curled against mine, just hours ago.

Glen is neatly stuffing her tightly rolled things into her rucksack. Everything will fit. She packed light because she always knew it was just a vacation. It is me that had other hopes, other ideas. Or, anyway, it is me who remained in denial, in non-thought, of this day.

"I wish you could stay," I say, hating the pleading in my voice.

She shakes her head, not meeting my gaze, "I can't. I have responsibilities back home, Liz. Christmas is one of our busiest times. And, I have no income here, I can't work, and you can't be supporting me."

When I start to protest that I can, and will, she rephrases, "I can't have you supporting me. You already work too much and I am home alone all day, doing nothing other than watch you burn yourself out."

Her words are so familiar.

This time, however, the remorse sounds mostly believable.

I don't have anything to say that I haven't already said. My words are also familiar, now.

Is that all my life is built on? Familiar words?

She stops her packing and comes to sit beside me on the bed. She takes my hand, "We'll be alright. I know this is difficult."

I don't know if she means we will be alright, together, or individually, as we each go our separate ways.

I stare down at our intertwined fingers, not wanting to meet her eyes and have her see the sadness in mine, or maybe it is because I can't stand to see that there is not this sadness in hers. "It's just... these past few weeks have been..." I lose my words. "Going back to normal is going to be hard."

This is the understatement of the century.

She tilts my chin up, forcing me to look in her eyes and kisses me softly. "Then don't go back," she murmurs against my lips, "Come to England with me instead."

I want to protest. I want to tell her that isn't an option.

But the spark of hope inside me is telling me something else. What if I *could*? What if I just packed it up and left with Glen instead of working non-stop to pay tuition and bills I can't afford and spending any downtime I do find drinking and going to bars.

She squeezes our laced fingers reassuringly, "I know it's a big decision. Just think about it? I don't want this to end if it doesn't really have to."

With that, she hops off the bed, packs the final items into her bag and zips it closed resolutely.

"I don't want to leave things like this between us," she says quietly, looking down at her bag for a long minute before shifting her gaze back to me, "but my ride is waiting and I have to make this flight."

I nod, not trusting myself to speak. I stand to say goodbye. She crosses the room and embraces me. We stand this way for several minutes, taking as much comfort from our tight hug as we can get. I won't go to the airport with her, for multiple reasons.

And, goodbye will be easier from here.

Eventually Glen pulls back just enough to catch my eyes, "This is hard, but I think we will see each other again, maybe even very soon?"

Her eyes search mine.

I want to believe that she will return, when the holiday season is over and the pace at the pub slows down, or that I can follow her, even if just for the Christmas break from university. I want to believe that either of us — both of us — want that to happen.

But I don't know, for certain, what either of us really do want.

I decide I will believe that we can make this work, that we want to make this work. In fact, I will believe both in her coming back and in me going to England.

Managing a small smile, I reply, "We'll make it work. I'll look into coming to visit you in England, over the holiday break..."

Glen smiles back, kissing me softly, then urgently, then breaking off the kiss and towing her bag out of the room. I do not follow, but listen as she goes up the stairs and out the door, which I hear clomp shut behind her.

* * *

For days, the thought of going to England swirls in my exhausted mind. I can barely sleep. I barely have time to sleep, with work not taking a holiday break and, with it being the final week of the university semester, all my assignments are suddenly due. But, when I do have a moment to doze on the bus during one of my commutes, I can't stop thinking about Glen's offer to join her in England. We have chatted a couple times since she left — in the short windows where the time zones align with our work schedules — and the reality is that I am pretty sure I won't be able to expect her to return here, at least not anytime soon. Not that I would be able to afford that in any case.

The opportunity to break free from this exhausting, meaningless life and be with Glen in a new place — without all the stress — is so tempting I am convinced I should already have bought my ticket. And, just before I commit to doing just that, reality reminds me I'd be throwing away everything I have built toward. If I abandon my graduate program, what would I do next? What would I do with my life, my career, my future?

I struggle through the final class of the semester in a distracted haze. I am only here in class because my semester final papers are due today and I want to be certain they are received on time.

After I hand in my final formal paper for this semester, Cherry and I meet with our thesis advisor where I drop off my end-of-term thesis update report. Cherry still has to complete hers, and needs a copy of mine in order to do so.

Cherry follows me to the graduate lounge where we both flop onto a couch.

I feel myself sink into the cushions. Dread and exhaustion battling to drown me.

Cherry peers at me, "I'm worried about you. You look totally wiped."

I exhale slowly, feeling raw and fragile. How can I explain any of this to Cherry, to anyone? My voice comes out thin, "I'm sorry, It's just —" My lip trembles and I bite it, willing back the sheen I feel coming to my eyes, "I feel... empty. Like everything I'm doing is just going through the motions. I can't even figure out what I want, in the end...— why am I even doing any of this?"

Her face softens. "You need to stop running yourself ragged.

Let's just sit here and people watch; stop thinking about work and school and... whatever it is that's taking all your energy. I am ready to listen, when — if — you want to talk."

"It's just... Glen, the woman I was seeing, went back to England..." I bite my lip again, imagining that I can still feel Glen's goodbye kiss. Cherry remains silent and waits for me to continue.

And then I spill it all — moving to Toronto, losing Toni, meeting Glen... the past few weeks with her, and now the temptation to just pack it all in, give up everything I have been killing myself to do for the past months, and just buy a ticket to England. A one-way ticket.

Cherry nods slowly, "I could tell you were struggling more in the past week or so, must be because of her returning to England. But this sounds deeper than just missing her."

Her words ring with truth. I hug myself, my arms tense and tight against my body. "It's everything all at once. Working so much with no free time, the stress of keeping up my grades, having no energy for anything anymore. And under it all, this hollow feeling like nothing really matters."

Tears trickle down my cheeks. Cherry pulls a tissue out of somewhere and hands it to me silently.

Eventually she squeezes my hand gently. "Hey, it's okay to not be okay. You've been running non-stop for so long with no break. No wonder you're burnt out."

"I don't want to make the wrong choice. But I don't know that I have any choice, really. I just don't think I can do this anymore." I say softly as I wave my arm around in front of us, at the room.

She sighs. "You've worked so hard, here, to get here, to get this far. Is there no other way to make it work? Can you move somewhere cheaper, or get a student loan, or, call your family, or something to take some of the pressure off? It would suck to give up on your dreams because of stress based on finances..."

I don't tell her that I have never really known what my dream is, that I have just been floating through the steps I thought were the appropriate ones for me, but that I have no idea what kind of future I want. I think, if I had a dream, that would make this whole process of sacrifice easier. Without a dream, however, what is the point?

Then Cherry offers a small, sad smile, "But, then, maybe a break is exactly what you need."

I nod mutely.

She adds, "Anyway, you have a decision to make, but know that I'll be here regardless of whatever path you do take."

I know that I can't keep drowning forever and expect to resurface. It is time to stop and breathe, or let the emptiness swallow me whole, for good.

Before her kindness undoes me further, I leave her on the couch as I head back toward the bus stop. I check my watch and realize I do have enough time to stop at the library and use one of the student computer stations to video call Glen, and still get home in time to get changed and head off to my night job.

Glen is is five hours later than me and is likely at work already, but I hope she will be able to take a short call. I only have 20 minutes to talk anyway. The five hour time difference makes our schedules almost completely incompatible.

As Glen's face loads on the screen, relief mingles with longing at seeing her. "Rough day?" she asks.

I guess my exhaustion is evident even through the laggy connection.

"Yeah, well, not so different from the last few months, actually. Hah."

She nods sympathetically. "I have had a long couple days too — the pub has been so busy with the Christmas dinner reservations that I have been working splits in the kitchen, and then hopping onto the bar until closing. These hours are killing me!"

"I bet. I wish we weren't so far apart..." I imagine I can feel the weight of Glen's hand wrapping mine.

Then a blurry figure passes behind Glen, and I hear a female voice, "Glen, can you help in the kitchen please, I'm swamped."

I don't wait for Glen to excuse herself, "Go. It's okay. I have to catch a bus anyway."

Her face scrunches and she sighs, "Yeah. I gotta go. I will try to call you tomorrow, after you get home, before I head in to work. Assuming I don't get called in for lunch again. Sigh... too bad all this business can't spread out over the entire year and not all come at the same time..."

"Until tomorrow then. Try to have a good evening. I am heading home now..." My voice breaks on the last words and I disconnect the call.

One Tequila, Two Tequila...

BAD PLACE TEQUILA

I walk into Petals, hoping, and intending, to make the most of whatever drink is on happy hour pricing, for as long as it is on happy hour pricing. But as I make my way through the crowded space toward to the bar, I am surprised to see Cherry sitting at the back end of the the bar, with an empty stool next to her. She has a stack of notes in front of her, but isn't looking at them. She is sitting sideways on the stool, watching my approach. She smiles as I get closer. I wonder at the tiny charge that runs down my chest as I appreciate how her smile has lit up her face.

"Heyyyyy..." Cherry drags out the word as I approach. I glance at her nearly empty glass and wonder how much she has had to drink. "You look like you can use a drink! What's your poison tonight...?" She gestures at the bartender.

The sign on the back of the bar indicates that tequila shooters are tonight's special.

"Looks like tequila." I hold up three fingers at the bartender who nods. "Works out well since it looks like I need something short and sweet to catch up to you."

Cherry giggles. "Two to kill yas, please, James."

The bartender, whose name is probably not anything like James, pours two more shots into Cherry's glass and waits for me to take a sip out of the glass she had set in front of me before topping it up with a generous pour. I pay her and she heads back to the front of the bar, still carrying the tequila bottle.

"Rough day?" I ask Cherry the question everyone I speak to seems to want to ask me.

"Meh. A day. Is yours going as shitty as mine? That why you're here?"

"My day has been a rough week..." I slide onto the stool next to her.

"How are you holding up, with Glen gone? Get any better now that you're done your papers for the semester?" she asks.

I shrug. "Who knows? If I were to answer out loud, I would say we are working on navigating the long distance waters — but if I share my real thoughts? — I would have to admit I wonder if we are just trying to figure out if we even want to navigate this..."

I wonder at my own candor, at this unexpected truthfulness. I backpedal, "Anyway, we are trying, and I am keeping it together... still working a lot, but, yeah, having my papers done for the semester is a huge relief."

Cherry just continues staring at me with big hazel eyes.

They are greener tonight than I have seen them before.

"It's fine. Really. She might be back in the new year, after the Christmas rush. She's busy this time of year, at the pub, and it's her job. She can't work here, so..." I trail off as Cherry squeezes my hand before releasing it and placing both her hands on top of the notes in front of her. Her glass is empty.

I have the strange impression that I can still feel Cherry gripping my hand.

I nod at the small pile of papers in front of her. "Hopefully you'll be done soon too." I tug a sheet out from under her hands. It contains some handwritten notes and a diagram. "Yeah. I am glad I am done my fall semester draft. I don't envy you still having to make sense of all this."

She slides the paper back from me, her fingers brushing my hand very lightly. My skin tingles at the contact. I make eye contact. She holds my gaze. Some silent conversation takes place. No words are needed — there is some silent detailed communication happening without any need for language.

I find myself studying Cherry's features, strong, serious... beautiful...

Her eyes don't leave mine.

I find myself...

"Oh for fuck sake." I pop off my seat suddenly and stand up. "Our drinks are empty. You want something different?" I wave at the bartender.

Am I imagining this chemistry, this charge between us?

How can I be?

A weird connection thrums in the breath or two that passes before she responds, "Sure, rum and coke."

The next section of time passes quickly. Cherry wraps up her thoughts and folds her notes away into her shoulder bag, and we people watch and chat, with our drinks on a regular refill rotation — her then me then her then me. When our knees bump under the bar top — more frequently than one might expect — a jolt of electricity sparks through my body, equal parts pleasurable and unsettling. I wonder if this is fully accidental. I wonder if I am bumping her, or she is bumping me. And, what does that mean if one of us is? If both of us are?

I catch Cherry looking at me oddly, I blurt out, "Dance with me?"

And just as I finish asking her, the music changes to a slow song.

Cherry smiles crookedly and nods. She moves ahead of me, toward the dance floor. I follow.

I stagger slightly as I sidestep to avoid a sitting woman who has just pushed her chair out from a table and bump into a second woman sitting beside her at the table.

The second woman turns sideways and looks up at me, "Oh, hi Liz."

"Violet." I reply, a wash of dread running down my back.

She looks in the direction I was heading. "You here with someone?"

I shake my head. Then I nod. "Well, sorta. I'm here with someone from university. She's doing a project and wanted to see... well, I'm doing a project and she wanted to see how I see my project..."

Violet just looks at me.

"Oh, nevermind. I don't think I understand the point of her project anyway. Something to do with the observed being the observer. Or maybe that's the other way around..."

I nod toward Cherry who is swaying to the slow music, by herself, on the floor, watching me, "Well. See you around."

She grabs my arm and holds onto it, "Are you seeing her?"

I snort. "No. She's straight."

Violet examines me closely, and looks over at Cherry on the dance floor. "Is she now..."

I extricate my arm from Violet's grip and join Cherry. We fumble awkwardly for arm placements for a moment, and giggle at each other before finally settling on both of us encircling the other's waist. Our bodies press close, as we sway together.

I think I can feel her heart pounding rapidly.

Is it because of me?

Is it me?

Doubt and want and alcohol race within me — I don't want another mistake on my plate, but there is some... attraction... here. Some overwhelming urge to... what? Go home with a straight woman?

It's the alcohol. I shake my head.

Then the song ends. Cherry meets my gaze. Slowly, giving me time to pull away, she leans her head toward me. But I'm the one who closes the final distance, capturing her lips with mine, tentatively at first, then deepening the kiss as she responds.

She tastes of rum, and longing, and forbidden and inappropriate, yet so right in this moment. One of her hands slides up my back to cup the back of my neck while the other plays across my lower back, pressing our bodies closer. Lost in sensation, and in the taste of her mouth, I let myself get swept away.

But then, as bodies around us start moving to the faster music, someone bumps into me and reality crashes back over me like a cold shower. My life is a mess. My relationship status is a mess. I am a mess.

I must be using Cherry as an escape, to distract me from my stress, my exhaustion, my inability to make decisions. It wouldn't be fair to either of us to start something in such a messy state.

I break our kiss and take a step back, breathing hard, "Cherry, I... I can't. It's... I am not in a good place. You don't want to be here, like this, with me."

Her eyes are dark again — the green in them nearly completely returned to a light brown hazel — but she nods in understanding. "You're right. Probably I am not in a great place right now either. I don't want to mess things up, or make anything worse, for either of us."

Our evening is over now. I find myself terribly disappointed.

"Probably we should head out — it's been a long evening. We've had a lot to drink. Look at what we almost got ourselves into!" She laughs and pats my shoulder. "Yeah, let's get out of here. The fresh air will sober us up."

Outside, she stops me before I head down the subway steps for my trip home. "You know I'm here if you need anything, right? Whether you want to vent or just hang out and take your mind off things for a while."

I smile, "Thanks Cherry, I appreciate the offer."

"I mean it. My door is always open if you need it," she says earnestly. She pauses, as if wanting to say more but is holding back.

Our eyes hold each other's for a long moment — a very long moment that does not move into the uncomfortable — an unspoken understanding passing between us. Cherry breaks this moment by turning and walking away.

I miss her presence immediately.

A Moment of Truth

WHERE'S THE UNDO BUTTON

I SIT ALONE in the corner of the dimly lit Petals. Some warmish golden liquid sloshes around my glass as I lift it to my lips. It burns its way down my throat and settles even more warmly in the pit of my stomach, muffling out the sharp pain that has engulfed me since... Glen left? Toni left? Since I left home? I slip a small bottle of cheap whiskey out of my pocket and use it to refill my drink glass. No matter how much I drink, it's never enough, and I can't afford drinks from the bar. Certainly not now that I lost my weekend night shift job. Lost? Or gave up — anyway, I am done there.

I absentmindedly swirl what remains of the liquid around inside the glass before gulping back another mouthful. I force my gaze away from the now empty glass, turning it toward the other side of the bar instead.

Violet looking back at me, jolts me. I fumble in my coat pocket for the next miniature bottle. And twist the lid off one handed. I don't look away from Violet. She is at a table with two other women. As soon as she looks at one of them, I hold my glass under the table and dump the contents of the bottle into it.

I want to not look at Violet again, to not catch her eye, but I can't stop myself. I look toward her table again. And she is walking toward me. My heart flops. I start to push my chair back from the table, to slip out from behind it, to run off... to the bathroom perhaps, then sneak out the door and head... somewhere. Maybe to Sapphics.

But I am too slow, probably too drunk, and trapped in the corner of the room so I cannot slip away, to the toilets, or elsewhere, past Violet because she is standing directly in front of me. She doesn't speak, just stands there, all four and a half feet of her solid little self, and stares at me.

I focus my gaze back onto the glass in front of me. The silence between us is tense, but eventually, she scrapes the chair next to me out from the table and sits. "Been seeing a lot of you recently, huh, Liz." She pretends to look around. "Where's your little British biscuit?" She emphasizes 'biscuit' like it is something slimy.

I look up into her eyes. I feel nothing but emptiness — there is not even a spark of hope that everything might eventually turn out alright. Smiling slightly, I nod before bringing my glass up in a toast, "I went low-carb, no biscuits."

"And your other friend is... straight...?"

I nod and swallow most of my drink.

She hadn't brought a drink over with her, but is quick to complete a round-trip to the bar and return with drinks for both of us. She slides a tall glass toward me, "Looks like whiskey to me, so that's what I got you. The bartender didn't know what you were drinking." She looks pointedly at my old, now empty, glass.

I accept the new drink. The taste of bitterness coats my tongue and I know this is not the whiskey's fault. The whiskey does, however, promise me a refuge from reality, so I drink it.

I imagine there is tension, between us, within her, within me. Different sources, different tensions, but all there.

Fortunately, alcohol has resolved most of that, from my point of view.

It has resolved me.

We drink. I drink. She talks. I cannot listen, but she talks anyway. She does not require responses from me, or, anyway, she does not appear to require anything more from me than what I am providing, which seems to be a body, at a table, in a bar.

The room pulsates with the bass-heavy beats of the DJ. This music sounds distant, muffled, muddled, but the rhythm of it is clear: heavy, hard, hurting. It suits me just fine.

* * *

I recall another, and then, maybe, another, clink of our glasses as our space becomes more cramped and other women join us at our table and they talk and dance and drink and sweat and dance some more. I don't dance. My legs are not secure enough for that. Violet sits with me. I watch the women come and go from the table to the dance floor, to the bar, and back. Time slips. The amber liquid swirls.

* * *

I wake up in a strange bed, the room shrouded in dim light. The curtains are closed but it looks like daylight seeps in through the tiny sliver where the curtains meet. The smell of stale alcohol lingers. I think it is from me. My head swims as I sit upright. I breathe shallowly so I don't get sick on the floor at the side of the bed. My mouth tastes like sour breath, and... sex. My stomach roils again.

I sit gingerly on the edge of the bed. The sheets beneath me are rough against my skin. I am naked. The room is messy and pretty clearly shows what occurred last night — discarded clothes, a lidless half empty bottle of Grey Goose vodka on the bedside table, and the lump of a stranger's body on the other side of the bed. A heavy weight settles on my chest and I have to swallow several times to keep whatever is in me from coming out.

The stranger stirs beside me as I survey the room slowly, to distract myself from my queasiness. My mouth is dry and I can't swallow properly. I can't seem to swallow away that weight in my chest. Feeling fully detached from myself, I can't decide if I want to — if I should — recall some details of last night. If what I feel now, this film of shame and revulsion, and this taste in my mouth that I am certain is not just from last night's drinking, represents last night, then... I don't want to know. Whatever it was, it has not made me feel any better, about anything, and especially about myself. It didn't even provide much of a distraction, at least, not a distraction I couldn't have created on my own, with a bottle, and no stranger in a bed next to me.

The taste of regret lingers on my tongue, bitter and unyielding, so I pick up the Grey Goose bottle and drink from it directly. It soothes my dry throat. It sanitizes my mouth. I need both, right now, immediately. My stomach seems to settle. I have another drink. And another. I set the bottle back on the night stand.

"Good afternoon." Her voice startles me. I glance at the stranger.

Violet, of course. It would have to be her.

But I knew — had known — it was her as soon as I swallowed the first mouthful of vodka from the bottle on the bedside table. I knew it was her even though her face, even now, is still obscured in the shadows of this dimly lit room. I knew.

I swallow another long mouthful of vodka from the bottle.

I don't speak. The silence between us draws out the emptiness that is swallowing me. The touch of her hand on my shoulder makes me cringe, inside, and leaves me cold. She tugs me backward into the bed.

I lie on my back and stare at the ceiling. I know she won't care if I pay attention. Her hand brushes up my belly. Her palm is rough, chapped, harsh. Or is that just my imagination, how I expect her touch to feel? I ignore her. She slides over me, holds herself up, her tits hanging low against me. I can smell her scent. I swallow my bile.

One of her thighs slips between mine. She rocks against me. The weight of her, the pressure of her cunt rubbing against me, hurts.

And she finally grunts against the base of my neck. Finally.

* * *

As I slip out of Violet's bed sometime later, the cool floor beneath my bare feet is a very stark contrast to the hellish warmth of the bed, of her in the bed. Of my shame. Of my degradation.

What have I done?

I shiver. I would rather freeze out here than crawl back in there. I will freeze before I do this again.

The thought brings tears to my eyes.

A void gapes within me. The scent of Violet's sex lingers on my face, in my nostrils. I slip into her bathroom and wash my face with her bar of hand soap, scrubbing hard with my fingertips, even up into my nostrils.

But it's a scent that doesn't so easily wash away. Fainter now, with a perfumed soap residue covering it, it remains as a reminder of what I have done.

I return to the bedroom and dress in silence, the rustle of fabric punctuating the quiet. Violet watches me, I think. I don't look at her, the weight of what I have done has settled like a chunk of rock in my stomach and I cannot look at her.

The city outside is noisy, awake, stinking of exhaust fumes and city air and of another evening getting ready to start with sounds of life and purpose and future that seem to mock me. I step into the early evening dusk, the sun already long faded behind cloud cover and early winter darkness. The cool breeze carries the scent of garbage, piled high in front of the restaurant beside Violet's apartment. The bleakness within me lingers at the edges of my consciousness. I wonder if a drink would help.

But I have to confront the wreckage of my life — a life that has become disconnected. A life that no longer really feels like my own. A life that just keeps expanding this emptiness inside me.

It will swallow me.

I think I can hear my the sounds of my own footsteps echoing even though the streets are busy with people going somewhere to do something that is meaningful to them. I navigate these unfamiliar downtown streets to find a subway that will eventually get me home where I can shower and maybe wash this misery away.

* * *

The decision forms on the bus leg of the trip home. After getting out of the subway and waiting 20 minutes longer for a bus, something finally cuts through the foolishness in my head. I need to leave this life. There is no way I can keep doing this. I cannot wake up in Violet's bed again. Anyone's bed again. Maybe I am chasing after something impossible, something unreal, in England, but staying in my current life feels more impossible, more unreal — are there gradients of unreal? Maybe I will regret my decision, but, right now, hungover and sitting on a bus with just more hangovers and bus-sitting on the horizon, more Violet, more Violets... I need to chase after something that holds at least some promise of... meaning.

The decision to follow Glen to England solidifies. I know I can't keep — I don't even have — the life I was building anyway, so why struggle to keep it, to pretend I can keep it. Why not just go. I lose nothing important, just meaningless work to pay meaningless bills to go to university that I am too exhausted to succeed in. And rinse and repeat.

I step off the bottom step of the bus and walk the few feet to my door and unlock it and let myself in and descend the stairs to a place where I can shower and change and figure out how I can get to England.

Ghost of Season Present

As the plane taxis to its final stopping point, I am still excited and nervous and exhausted and exhilarated all at the same time. It has been a frantic week since I made my decision and bought my one-way airfare to England. And nearly a month since I watched Glen lug her bag out of my apartment and disappear.

I clear immigration quickly and, as I walk to the luggage carousel, I find myself relieved that I will now have some time to stop... to just stop for a while and look around.

And, then I see her. Glen is waiting with a beaming smile.

I blame the overnight flight and lack of sleep for the dullness I feel.

She hugs me. Then pulls her head back and looks at me. "You must be exhausted. It's a long flight from Toronto. Let's get out of here." She takes the pull handle of one of my bags and shifts it to her right side.

She presses her lips lightly and quickly against mine, then we separate, but she holds my hand firmly as we walk toward the exit doors. "I am parked in the short-term, just outside. Come on, let me show you around." I am not sure I hear excitement in her voice. Or in my own.

As Glen drives, she talks about the landmarks that we can't

actually see from the motorway, and tells me about some of the things that we can go sightsee once I get settled in. I stare out the window and half listen, half wonder at the amount of stone in the buildings and sidewalks and pathways through what look like small treeless parks. Half wonder at the weight inside me that has not yet lifted.

Eventually she pulls up around the side of a barn-shaped build-ing, also made of stone. A large sign out front, shaped like a crown, announces the pub's name: The Crown. "And this is home sweet home!" she announces proudly. She pulls my two bags out of the trunk and heads around the side of the building, wheeling them both behind her. I follow.

There is a door at the end of the building that opens into a small foyer with a set of stairs going up, and a door along a short hallway, to the left of the stairs. Glen moves aside for me to head up the stairs ahead of her and hands me the smaller of my two bags. She points to the door, "That's to the pub. It should be locked — it usually is — so the patrons don't make their way up here. Not that they would, but... you know... it's a pub."

The apartment on the second floor runs the length of the building. It has two small bedrooms along the front wall, over-looking the Crown sign. The rest is open, with a kitchenette sepa-rated from the main body of the living space by a long thin island. The place is small and tidy and very impersonal. I can't picture Glen making dinner in the kitchen nook. There are no windows. Unless the windows are in the bedroom. Which they must be, because you can't have an entire apartment with no windows.

It's odd that Glen seems to have not made this place feel lived in, let alone like she lives in it. I know she had been here in the village, working at this pub — with her ex, but I make myself not think about that — for nearly a year before she went to Canada so it should feel lived in.

She leads me to the bedroom closest to the stairs and waves me into the room, "This is the master suite."

She uses the term loosely. It is a small room with a double

futon for a bed. And a single chest of drawers. The closet is a metal clothing rail that is mostly full of button up shirts and black pants on pant hangers. There is a stack of boxes at the end of this clothing rail, with a face down wooden picture frame lying on top. I set my bag beside the boxes, the only space for it that is out of the way of the walkway into the room.

Some crazy urge has me flipping over the frame before I realize what I am doing.

It's a picture of a brunette with her arm draped over Glen's shoulder, both of them smiling into the camera.

Unease blooms in my gut. "Glen... is that Melanie?" I ask cautiously, but I know already that it is.

She sighs, "Yes, that's Mel. We were together for quite a while, before, you know that."

"Ummm, yeah, I know, but why do you still have photos of your ex around?"

Glen reaches for my hand reassuringly, "My personal stuff is still in those boxes. I never got around to fully unpacking... when Mel and I split, I moved in here and then, well, I was too busy taking trips across the ocean. That frame didn't fit in a box, I guess. I told you, Mel and I are just close friends now." Glen pauses, "She's been helping out at the pub too, while I was away in Canada... and, well, is still here just now, but she will be moving on soon."

She pulls me closer. "And, once you're trained up, they won't need her help in the pub anymore... and the bonus is that you'll have a job built in." She kisses me.

It takes me a second to process her words. My first thought was that I had thought Glen lived here in this place, with Melanie, before they split up, but, now, it seems they must have lived together, somewhere else — but that thought simply disappears when the second part of the conversation sinks in.

I pull back and stare at her, "Melanie is working here? Now?"

Glen sighs tiredly. "Please don't overthink this. I didn't mention it before only because I knew you'd overthink things if you found out Mel was here too. You didn't need more stuff on your plate. And she actually was here already, filling in while I was away in Canada. She has worked here for a long time too. There was no intention to keep anything a secret. I swear."

I don't know what to say, but before I can respond, a jaunty voice calls out, "Anyone home?"

Glen shoots me an apologetic look as she goes back to the living area. I follow her.

My stomach drops as soon as I step into the room and see none other than Melanie standing there with a tray of pastries and a carafe.

I wonder if the door to the pub was unlocked.

Or not.

Melanie's eyes narrow almost imperceptibly at the sight of me standing in the bedroom doorway, but she doesn't look at me long before focusing on Glen, "Thought you could use some food, for lunch, and... for your guest." I imagine I hear a strange emphasis on the word guest. She trails off, not bothering to even pretend she is going to acknowledge me, or that she knows my name. Which, of course, she must, since it appears she is practically living with Glen.

I grit my teeth into what I hope passes for a polite smile.

Glen takes the tray from her. "Thanks Mel, you're a lifesaver as always. Liz can probably use some coffee, it was a long flight."

Mel doesn't look at me. I walk over to the kitchen space where they are standing.

Like a repulsed magnet, Melanie backs away from us. "I gotta get back, it's busy down there."

And then it is just Glen and I in the apartment space.

The sensation of being a complete outsider nearly overwhelms me. The residue of Melanie's presence remains in the air around us.

Despite Glen's reassurances, I don't believe Melanie still working here in the pub is just because it was convenient. I know there is something still simmering between them, whether Glen admits it consciously or not. Or, perhaps, whether Glen realizes it or not — Melanie isn't here to help out the pub, or because she can't find other work, elsewhere... I know this. I don't know how I know this, but I know it. Melanie is not 'over it'.

But I am jet-lagged and tired and I drink the coffee and eat the pastries that Melanie brought and choose to ignore what I believe. I will carry on and hope I am imagining that I am competing with a real-life specter from Glen's past.

What choice do I have now?

A Month Later

THE PUB IS BUSTLING. I don't even have time to make small talk with the regulars, who come every day in the same time slots: the *immediately-after-work-and-before-heading-home* segment, the *take-the-little-woman-out-for-dinner* segment and the *have-a-few-downthepub-before-going-into-town-and-getting-into-fist-fights* segment.

I don't know what happened to the after-holiday lull Glen had predicted. I don't know what happened to having time to go sight-seeing, to heading to London for day trips, to going someplace where Glen and I could actually act like we knew each other in public.

This Friday night it seems as though the three pub crowds have overlapped. The *after-workers* have their wives with them, and are staying for meals, and the *downthepubbers* are out extra early, getting extra drunk.

Glen is in the kitchen, helping Melanie keep up with the food orders. I am trying to not think about Glen in the kitchen with Melanie so I will be able to keep up with the drinks and food orders. There isn't a better way to organize the team on this super busy night: I can't work with Melanie, well, *I* could work with her, she won't work with me. She has made that plenty clear over the past couple weeks during the clean ups at the end of the night when she leaves every area I enter about a step ahead of me actually entering. She must have some sixth sense.

I take another food order from a regular *bring-the-wifey* customer. I check nobody else is hanging at the bar looking to order drinks and slip out through the bar opening to run the food order into the kitchen. The kitchen door has a window at head level, so I can see Glen and Melanie standing close, along the prep counter side of the room. There should be no prepping emergency at this time of night that would require both cooks to be hovering there.

I push the swinging door inward and imagine that I see Glen step back quickly.

"Counting the veg?" I ask as I stop just inside the room.

"Just taking a moment, Liz, it's been pretty hectic in here tonight."

"Yeah, I can tell. I'm pretty hectic myself," I hear the tension in my voice.

Melanie doesn't take her eyes off me. But she speaks to Glen. "Why the fuck is she here. In here. No, actually, *here* at all…"

Glen shrugs dismissively and steps toward me with her hand out for the food order slip, "It's just work. We're all adults."

I am not sure who Glen is speaking to. Or about. And am about to ask when the bar bell that is supposed to be reserved for last calls starts ringing. Someone has to have let themselves behind the bar to ring it. "Shit." I stuff the food order into Glen's hand and swivel to head back out and ask the hooligan behind the bar to take a seat.

But I don't miss the anything-but-adult way Melanie's gaze lingers on me.

After the food menu is taken down for the night, the bar remains bustling so Glen switches to helping me on the bar, now that the kitchen is closed. We don't have time to chat with each other, but when we pass in the narrow space, and nobody is looking, we bump hips, or brush fingertips. The contact almost alleviates some of my worry.

Some time later, after Glen has been helping me on the bar for over an hour, I see Melanie sitting in a booth directly across from the bar opening, facing the bar. She stares unapologetically at me from there, a scowl etched into her features.

I try to remain focused and carry on conversations with patrons sitting at the bar, and ignore Melanie as best I can. Most of these patrons just want to chat with me so they can comment on my accent. If they were looking for drinks, instead of chatter, they would be asking Glen for service since she is much more efficient at pulling pints than I am.

I am chatting with a regular who is sitting at the bar, near the bar opening. My eyes are resting just beyond him, on Melanie. She is still staring at me. She casually gives me the finger.

In this battle of wills, I suspect she will win. I don't have the energy, the space, or the freedom, to make angry eyes. I fight the urge to return her finger gesture.

Glen seems oblivious to the simmering rage oozing from the booth. The regular I am talking to, however, is not. He glances at Melanie, then at me, then takes his beer and heads over to a seat near the pool table.

I shake my head and turn back toward the center of the bar.

"Yeah. You do that." Melanie's voice pokes me from much closer than the booth.

She has taken the seat the regular just vacated and is leaning on the bar top, both elbows planted. "What do you want, Melanie?" I know she can hear the exasperation in my voice, as I return to stand closer to her, on my own side of the counter.

It appears the beating around the bush phase is over between us.

But there is an audience here, a room full of witnesses that are watching us size each other up. Glen is not out, here, in her job, or in this community. This means I am not out here, in this community. Melanie, I had assumed, was also living in the closet, but tonight it does not appear that she is concerned about airing her personal issues in a public place. I can see out of the corner of my eye that the men — only men here at this hour — sitting on stools at the bar are looking our way. No doubt listening. My voice — my accent, most likely — stands out.

Then Glen physically steps between me and the counter, her back to Melanie, "Why don't you call it a night, I will close."

I walk away, through the bar opening, close enough by Melanie that I could, and nearly do, bump into her stool. The veneer of civility, of pretending heterosexual normalcy, wins. There is no way to relieve this tension in this space without revealing Glen's closeted secret.

I hear Melanie's hushed hiss, meant for Glen's ears, and likely for mine, only. "Well, I am so fucking baffled at your taste. What were you thinking? How desperate can you get? I hadn't thought you could have actually stooped lower, scraped lower down the barrel than that other Canadian... and low and behold..."

I don't stop. I don't ask what the hell she is talking about. I keep walking, fists clenched, nails biting into my palms, through the door to the kitchen, past it, through the door that is supposed to lock the pub out of our private life, and up the stairs to the live-in suite Glen and I occupy above the bar proper.

It is a couple hours, and a few drinks, later that I hear the door from the pub bang shut. A few moments pass before Glen emerges from the stairway into the living area of the apartment.

She looks exhausted.

I am beyond irritated by Melanie's behavior, and by my lack of ability to deal with it, or her, or to remove myself from her constant chafing presence. And with Glen's refusal to deal with it, or her.

Glen sits next to me on the couch. "It got pretty unpleasant down there..." she says quietly, glancing over at me. I nod silently.

"Well, anyway, Melanie won't be back. She has a new job, and she understands that this kind of... behavior... can't happen here.

We can't be having personal feuds in the pub. It will affect business, and we can't have that."

I manage a smile. It feels so fake I wonder how my cheeks can hold the shape. "Yeah, I understand." But, in my mind, I wonder how it came about that Melanie just decided to leave, just decided to go get a new job. "Was that why she was such a... twat... tonight? Because she was done here?" I ask.

Glen sighs. "Yes. I assume so. She knows better. She knows we have to hide being gay here. It isn't safe to be out. It isn't good for business..."

There is a weird unease in my gut. Something feels off about this whole situation, though I can't quite put my finger on it. But Glen leans in to me and kisses me and slides her hand under my shirt and then I stop thinking about Melanie completely.

Blast from the Past

It is a couple weeks later — a couple quiet and almost peaceful weeks, with Melanie gone without another peep — that a loud bang jerks me awake. Someone is banging on the front door. I glance at the clock — 3 a.m. "Who the hell..."

I climb out of bed and throw on Glen's robe. I scoot down the stairs quickly, toward the door leading to the back of the pub, the door that acts as our private entrance. If I turn right, I could enter the pub itself, and use that exit. But at 3 a.m., it is locked up tight.

The insistent knocking at the door, continues. I hear Glen shuffling behind me, still upstairs.

I peer out the peephole.

When I see Sierra standing there, swaying from side to side, clearly drunk, I literally shake my head and look again. How can Sierra be here, outside this door, knocking. How can she be here, in this country, let alone outside the pub door where Glen and I live.

I don't question her drunkenness, however. My stomach sinks. This makes no sense.

I don't know why she is here, but whatever reason she is here cannot be a good one. Sierra pounds on the door again, "I know you're in there, open up!"

I don't know how she is here. Why she is here. Who is she here for? And, again, the thought pulses, how can she be here, in England?

I weigh my options — ignore her pounding on the door, call the police and risk escalating things, when I have no idea what is going on, or try to diffuse the situation myself, and find out what the hell is going on. Ignoring her out there will not be a valid option, as her knocking continues. The nearest neighbor is a couple house lengths away, due to the presence of the village green adjacent to the pub, and the main road along the front of it, but Sierra's pounding will eventually attract attention. And, likely, the police too.

Reluctantly, I unlock the deadbolt.

Sierra shoves past me into the dark foyer. "Where is she?" she slurs, whirling to face me, the smell of booze practically rolling off her.

Then she freezes suddenly and stares at me. "What. The. Fuck. You? What are you doing here?"

I want to ask her the same thing, but, as she lurches toward me, I just step back, quickly.

"I need to talk to Glen," she slurs, trying to push past me to the stairs leading up into the space Glen and I share.

"Whoa, easy now," I block her calmly but firmly, "I think this conversation has to wait, until sometime when you're sober."

"Fuck off," Sierra spits. "I came all this way for closure and I'm not leaving until —"

"Sierra?" Glen's voice floats from behind me. I turn to see her standing on a step halfway down the stairs.

Sierra shoves past me abruptly. "Wow. You dragged her all the way here too? Needed someone else in your collection?" Sierra turns to face me. "I can't believe you were stupid enough to follow her here!"

"Let's calm down. You aren't making any sense."

She rounds on me, jabbing a finger in my face. "Don't you fucking tell me what to do!"

"Sierra! Come on. Come upstairs, I'll make coffee," Glen intervenes before I shove Sierra back and the situation escalates into some weird brawl between a couple of Canadians in a narrow foyer between the upstairs accommodations and the main floor of a pub in some tiny village in rural England.

Sierra deflates.

Almost literally, she deflates. And meekly walks up the stairs behind Glen. I follow and we manage to maneuver Sierra onto the sofa while Glen makes coffee with hands I could swear are shaking.

Once Sierra has finished her first cup of coffee, and is calmer, if not soberer, Glen starts speaking to her, directly, in hushed tones, "I'm sorry it ended the way it did. I never meant to hurt you."

Sierra tilts her head toward me and actually guffaws, "Oh, *Sweetie,* will you tell *her* the exact same thing... when she meets your ex and... well... you see where we are now."

My stomach plummets, and, wordlessly I brace against the kitchen counter, waiting to hear what she is bound to tell me.

Sierra speaks a lot more quietly, and more soberly, than I expected she could, "Guess I, um, have some bad news to tell you. About Glen." Sierra takes a breath, then speaks to me while staring at Glen, "When she first moved back here, Glen hooked up with Melanie. I am pretty sure she came back here because of Melanie, actually. That's who's she's been with all along, you know. We were just her Canadian intermissions. I was intermission one, you were number 2." Sierra breaks into a loud giggle. "Number 2! But not like, in the Star Trek way. More like in the bowel movement way..."

I grip the counter to stay upright, to stay in place, my mind reeling.

But am I truly surprised?

Glen looks at me and shakes her head 'no'. She doesn't speak.

"No. Sierra," I shake my head as well, "you're drunk and angry."

"Yeah. You're right. But that doesn't make me wrong." Sierra nods to herself. "Just thought you deserved to not be the only one who didn't know the truth of what's going on around here. God knows Glen won't be telling it to you." Sierra hiccups.

Glen just shakes her head sadly and looks at me. "She's drunk Liz, there is nothing in what she is saying. Melanie was working here, that's it. I already explained that."

I nod. Glen is correct.

I pour myself a drink and go sit on the far side of the room and let them talk. I am in some weird shocked state. I can't understand why Sierra is here in this country, let alone in the apartment I share with Glen, or how she knew where Glen was, and why she would come here... and...my thoughts don't stop.

Later, after Sierra is finally sober enough to leave, and make her own way to the train station to head home, to London apparently, I turn to Glen, confused, "You knew she followed you here to England and didn't tell me? Why the secrecy?"

Glen sighs wearily, "I didn't want to worry you. I never thought she would show up here. She wanted a fresh start and has been in London for a few months now, actually. She came here before I even came home in December... I guess my stories of England got her thinking she could have a different life here."

I am baffled. "Glen, I'm your girlfriend. Hiding things isn't okay. Why wouldn't you have told me she was in the country, at least? And what is this about Melanie? What was Sierra talking about?" There is so much wrong with this situation that I can't even think clearly about which aspect disturbs me more.

She nods, eyes bright. With guilt? "You're right, I'm sorry. I'll do better about communication, I am just not used to being open about things — that hasn't been part of my life, sharing my worries. And I didn't really know how, or even if I should mention that Sierra moved here..."

I am not sure I believe her. I am not sure, even if I did believe her, if that would ease this deepening worry in my belly. Worries. These deepening worries. The worries I didn't even know I needed to have. The worries about Sierra, about Melanie, about what Sierra thinks she knows about Melanie. About Glen?

Optional

WHEN I COME UPSTAIRS after my lunch shift, Glen is sitting at the small kitchen table. She motions for me to join her. Feeling awkward, I sit across from her, meeting her eyes. "What is it?" I ask cautiously.

She hesitates, biting her lip. "I got a call today... from an old friend in Manchester. She works for a large brewer company and they have an opening for an experienced bar manager at one of their pubs in Blackpool. The money is really good and it could be a great opportunity for me."

My stomach sinks as I process what she's telling me. "You're thinking of taking the job," I say slowly.

She nods. "This can't go on, here, like it is now, Liz," her eyes don't let go of mine. "I can't choose between you and my career. I can't live in the closet, and we can't be out here. I can't have the locals thinking I'm queer, that you're queer. It isn't safe for us, it isn't good for business. But I can't continue to live like this, you can't live like this either. It's not healthy."

"Yeah. That makes sense. I am not attached to being here, that's for sure — Manchester will be more interesting, to the tourist part of me." I feel a tiny bit of excitement about getting out of rural small village England to a bigger and busier city where we can actually come out of the closet and go out in public as a couple.

I hear the apology in her voice, "Ummm, I will have to go on my own for a month or so, to get settled into the job, and find a place. When I get there, I will have a room in the pub I am working in, but it's for staff only." She pauses for a second.

In that second, hope bottoms out in my belly.

A million thoughts race through my head at once. Blackpool is a couple hundred miles away — practically a whole other country from where we are now, at least by UK measures.

Glen continues, "I think it would only be a couple weeks, or maybe a month, before I find a flat for us. It won't be very long, and you can carry on working here in the meanwhile, so when you do come, you will have some extra money to sightsee Manchester. We'll only be an hour and a bit train ride outside of Manchester, which is huge. And way more gay friendly than this place."

While Glen talks excitedly about how great Manchester will be, I can't help wondering if there's something — or someone — else drawing her away. After all, it was only a very short while ago that Melanie was insulting Glen's taste and implying she could do better than me. And just last week, Sierra was doing pretty much the same.

It was not at all the same though, was it Liz, what Sierra was suggesting.

The skepticism must show on my face because Glen reaches out to take my left hand gently in both of hers, "I know this is a lot to process. And I wouldn't even consider it if I didn't think we could make this work." Her eyes search mine.

I don't pull my hand away. I struggle with restraining myself, but do succeed in maintaining my calm. I don't speak my thoughts: *do you, Glen? Or is this really just an easy way out of our relationship? An excuse to end things without having to be the bad guy?*

The question does not come out of my mouth.

"A couple weeks, huh," I say. I want a drink. "Manchester —

Blackpool — is quite a ways away. This could change... things. And it would be nice to live someplace a bit less homophobic... that certainly will be a weight off us." I force myself to look on the bright side — and to ignore the flip side: *why?*

"That's exactly it! I can get settled up there. It will only be a couple weeks, and you can come up. It won't be too long and I will have enough money to get our own little flat, which won't be connected to the pub we work in, and you can come up and we won't have to live in the closet like we do here."

The rest goes unsaid — we don't have to specify the real pressures on us and our hidden relationship caused by the lack of acceptance in this small community. And, we don't have to mention that we have done this before, in the period after she came home to the UK while I was wrapping up my university semester. In that period where I wasn't certain I should pack in my life as I knew it to come across the ocean to be with a woman who I had known for only a couple months — when I wasn't certain I wanted to do that.

In *that* period... that period I have never discussed with Glen. Could not bring myself to discuss with Glen. A period that is still fresh in my head, and I think — some of it anyway — is fresh in hers too. That period, I suspect, is the reason behind why I have not pressed Glen to explain Sierra's presence in England, or Melanie's here at the pub...

Glen seems to understand my doubts because I think I see her posture soften as she squeezes my hand. I fight the unexpected urge to pull it away. "I know it will be difficult. But we can make this work, we did when you were still in Canada. And it won't be very long anyway — just until I get settled, maybe a couple weeks..."

Her optimism would be reassuring if not for the ton of doubt pressing into me. "Hopefully it won't take long to get settled," is what I say out loud, but what I think is: *what if you get settled into your new life in the city and decide this... us... isn't really what you want anymore? What if that is precisely why you want to get settled in a new place...*

My voice cracks on my last words as sudden panic rises in my chest.

I gave up everything for her. I gave up my life, and my future, and my country and I am living in a small homophobic community and pretending I am straight, for her. Doing all that and still being alone, still feeling alone, and the idea of going through another breakup, in this situation, is almost unbearable.

Her eyes hold mine earnestly. "All I know is that I care deeply for you and I want to make this work, and I don't think we are doing ourselves justice living here."

"Okay," I say finally, taking a deep breath. "Let's give this a try."

I don't know what my other option is.

<h1 style="text-align:center;font-style:italic">Two Bags Full</h1>

It's over two weeks later, nearly into the third when Glen determines it is okay for me to come see her — to see the apartment she finally found, and visit with her in her new life. It will be another couple weeks before I move up to join her, but this trip will provide me with a sense of what I am moving to.

I am eager to move to be with her, to see about setting up a life together where we are actually able to be together. I would have preferred to just pack up my stuff, what little I have, and take it in my two bags with me now, and just stay there with her while I get adjusted to the new locale and find myself a new job, but she thought I should give notice at the pub, and not go without the income just yet, since she was just getting on her feet there.

It did make sense. I don't have a work permit, and cash jobs are limited mostly to pub work, so it might take a bit of time for me to find a pub who was willing to bend the employment rules in exchange for a Canadian accent behind the bar.

I ignore, as much as I can anyway, the distance I feel when I chat with her. She has not gotten internet yet because she works all the time, so I haven't even seen her on video calls since she left. And our phone calls are short and always interrupted by one or the other of us having to return to work. She says she is just tired from the long hours and that it will pass once she is more settled in to the new routine.

She doesn't mention how she might expect things to change based on my pending arrival.

I know that, while this trip is just for this weekend, I will be moving for good in only a couple weeks. I know that we were apart for longer when I was still in Canada and she was here. What I don't know is why the nerves in my belly, now, are so much worse.

I feel so disconnected — so distant. It's so much worse now than when I was an ocean's distance away.

I tell myself it is just because, here, she is my only connection. Back in Canada I had work and university and — I shake Cherry's face out of my head —... friends.

I make my way to the address of the apartment — flat, here, I guess I need to start calling it — Glen has moved into. It is only a short walk from the train station. I didn't arrange for Glen to meet me at the station because there were two train connections to get here, and there was no way to let her know if any of the trains were delayed, or if I made both connections. And it is only a short walk and one corner to turn to find the address so getting lost wasn't really a concern.

I knock on the apartment door without even attempting to check if it is locked. I feel like a stranger, after only two weeks. Like an intruder, almost.

As if she was standing just on the other side of the door, Glen pulls the door open. "Liz!!" She embraces me tightly but I wonder if I imagined, in the quick glimpse I had of her before the hug, that her smile seems strained.

The reason for her speed in answering the door quickly becomes apparent as she takes me on a tour of the flat by standing inside the door and waving her arm around the one room kitchen-dining-living area. To our right are two doors, one that tucks in behind the wall that forms the kitchen and the other next to it, at a right angle. They are so close together I don't think one could open both doors at the same time. She points to the door behind the kitchen wall, "That's the loo." And swings the other door open to show the bedroom. It has a neatly made double bed, and the door just clears the foot of it to swing fully open.

The place feels uninhabited. But Glen hasn't even been here three weeks, and just got this place last week. So probably it makes sense for the place to feel so clinically bare.

"Sorry the place is so bare, I have been working late shifts and a lot of splits, so I really just crash here."

I want this explanation to ease my mind, but it does not.

We go for dinner at the pub where she has been working. It's a Saturday evening and the dining room is not overly busy. It doesn't look any busier than the pub Glen left working at, at home, with me.

The bar, however, is quite a bit busier, It's only 6, and all the bar stools are occupied. They must have a lot more regulars.

Glen notices me noticing. "It's the tourists. Lot of people come here for their holidays, well, lots used to come here I guess, Blackpool has become less popular now that travel to Europe is so easy and cheap. Back in the day this was the place to go on holiday... But anyway, yeah, the wives are probably out shopping for trinkets or playing the penny machines, or whatever, and the husbands nip in here for a pint. You should see the prices too, half as much again as out East."

We are seated in the dining room on the far side of a giant fireplace with an extra wide stone chimney that separates the dining area from the bar seating area. I can only see the bar area through the openings on either side of the stone-surrounded fireplace. The waitress brings us our gin and tonics from the closer of the two openings. We clink glasses after the waitress departs with our food order. "To table service then!" I cheers Glen, "so I won't have heart failure over the pricing of drinks."

We both giggle, and finish our drinks. When the waitress swings past our table on her way back to the kitchen with the order from the next table Glen asks for two more. "I get a staff discount, so the prices aren't too bad, for us anyway."

It isn't long after we finish our second drinks that the waitress brings over our food and sets the plates in front of us. Pub food from the specials' board never takes long. That's why it's on the specials' board, it's all pre-made and sitting on the pass table in the kitchen, waiting to be sent out. If it cools too much during its wait, there's a microwave beside the pass that will warm it up just fine. I have been spending a lot of time helping out in the kitchen at the Crown, since the owner did not replace either Melanie or Glen when they each left. While there was a longer than usual post-holidays busy time, it did turn out that Glen was correct in saying that pub trade dropped off quite dramatically in the winter months.

Working in a kitchen is definitely something I never thought I would be doing, as I am, overall, a terrible cook, but it turns out reheating shepherd's pie in a microwave isn't that difficult.

The waitress returns, with another round of gin and tonics for us. She smiles privately at Glen. There is something excessively familiar about this smile, and when the smile Glen returns looks sheepish, a twinge of suspicion shoots through me.

"Do you two work together often?" I ask the waitress.

"I do mostly the lunch shifts, actually. Not so much the evenings. But, yeah, I do see Glen here quite a bit." The waitress doesn't hesitate in her response.

Glen barely meets my eyes, overly focused on her food. The waitress wanders off.

I silently ask her to look at me. She does not, so I speak. "Glen?"

She heaves a long sigh. "I have to tell you something. Don't overreact though."

My heart pauses a beat.

Literally. It pauses for a beat.

She looks over toward the bar area. I follow her gaze, waiting for her to say more.

Then, she doesn't need to say more.

Because that's when I see her — Melanie — standing behind

the bar in a flattering black shirt, smiling broadly as she mixes some fancy cocktail with practiced ease.

My heart sinks along with any remaining optimism.

Glen never bothered to mention that Melanie moved up here too. Or, even, with her? And that oversight tells me all I really need to know.

Melanie — behind the bar. Working. Looking over at us, sitting here at this table in a pub in Blackpool.

Fury and betrayal ignite a fire somewhere low in my belly that burns out any words I might have had and it takes a minute, or two, before I can speak again.

"Glen. What the fuck?" I demand coldly "Are you seeing her? Is that what this is? You moved here to have a relationship with your ex-girlfriend, oh, well, my bad, not *ex* it seems, after all."

"Liz, it's not what you think. I was going to tell you, I swear."

My heart pulses in my neck. "So this is all... what? You're mocking me? Humiliating me? Why? I don't understand why you had me come up here..."

"She wasn't supposed to be working tonight. I wouldn't have brought you here to the pub if I had known."

"Oh, so. I was to be your side piece? I come up for a weekend boff, then go home — oh, sorry, back East to the Crown, my home isn't here, after all, is it — like a good little... what?"

Tears burn my eyes. "How long have you been fucking her?"

"It's not like that, I promise!"

"How long, Glen. Did you move here to be with her?"

Glen stares sadly at her hands. "No. I didn't know she was going to come here. She kinda followed me. I didn't plan this. I would never intentionally hurt you like that, I..."

"Don't." My voice trembles with rage and hurt. All this bull-shit. All her flimsy excuses... they are so clearly lies now. "How long? How long have you lied to me?"

Glen hesitates before mumbling, "Just a few days. She just got here a few days ago. Honest..." Glen sighs heavily, draining her glass. "Melanie ended up getting a job here too. We work together a lot — most of our shifts."

My blood runs cold at the look on Glen's face.

"And?" I prompt, dread pooling in my stomach.

She meets my gaze steadily. "I know I said there was nothing there, anymore. And I did mean that. But working with her has made me realize some feelings never really went away. I think I still have some for her."

The world tilts violently under my feet. This can't be happening.

I push away from the table and stand on shaking legs.

"So what does this mean for us?" I hate how small my voice sounds. How simple I sound. I know what this means. I am not stupid. I don't know why I ask.

Glen fiddles with her now empty glass, fully avoiding eye contact. "I can sort through this, I know it. I just need a bit of time... to get my head straight."

"Isn't that what you're already supposedly doing? Up here, living in a shithole apartment, working all the fucking time! Or, telling me that's what you're doing." I realize I am shouting and stop, suddenly. There is no point in this.

She keeps talking but the rest of her words fade into the white noise buzzing in my ears.

I drain my drink and drop the empty glass back on the table where it topples onto its side and rocks gently.

Melanie crosses the dining room and stands next to the table, next to Glen, almost directly across from me. "You know," she says in a low voice, "Glen was never really yours to begin with. Nobody knows why you came here, that was so stupid. You are old enough to know better, aren't you?" She looks me up and down, then shrugs and adds, her words mean and intentional, "Probably doesn't matter anyway, from what I understand I'm sure you'll find someone else soon enough."

I walk past her as if I hadn't heard her. My mind is focused on a single, unemotional thought: get out, now. Go.

I walk out. Through the dining room, past the bar, out into the cold night air.

I hear Glen trailing behind me. She keeps up with me as I walk briskly back to her nearby apartment.

The apartment door clicks shut. I step away from her. She stands still, just inside the door. "For fuck's sake Glen, why? Why did you do this to me? Why have me come up here at all? She moved here for you, didn't she?"

Or did you move here for her? But I don't ask that. I don't think I need to. I don't think the answer matters in any case.

"Maybe she did. But it's not what you think, I swear! We haven't done anything." Glen pleads, palms up in a surrendering gesture.

My bitter laugh startles even myself, "Then explain how this works then, because from where I'm standing, it looks like you moved up here to be with your ex who you just admitted you still have a thing for, all while stringing me along in some tiny shitty homophobic village as your secret backup — what, piece? Side dish... security blanket in case good ol' Mel doesn't work out?"

"That's not fair! I just want to close the chapter between Mel and I — we have a history and I don't think I had fully resolved that... I think that stands in our way — yours and mine. Yes, I still care for her but she and I don't work. I didn't cheat on you — that's not who I am. You know that..." She grips my wrists.

I shake her off. "No, you're right — cheating isn't you, not directly anyway. But having your cake and eating it too clearly is. You want me tucked safely away in some closet while you 'sort yourself out'? That's so..." I stumble on the words. I have no words for how horrible this is. I gave up everything on the belief, the hope — the dream — that I could have something with Glen, in a new world... a world where I didn't have to worry about what I am going to do for a living, and with whom I can share that life.

I have to clear my throat. I can't speak through my anger.

Or through my hurt? My hurt over this giant lie which has drawn me away from my education, my country, my future.

Glen reaches for me again pleadingly, "Please don't. I love you, you have to believe that. Just give me a chance to make this right — I will go home with you tomorrow, and stay, so we can work through this." Her eyes search mine desperately.

But I've already decided.

I step back out of her reach.

"No, I think not believing you is exactly what I need right now. I will leave tomorrow. Tonight you can fuck off to somewhere. Go to Mel's." I look around the apartment. "Unless she was staying here, in which case the two of you can fuck off to somewhere. I don't care. There are no trains tonight to get me home..." I grunt bitterly, "Well, yeah, to Norwich I mean, it is perfectly clear that was never really meant to be home, for me anyway."

My steady tone surprises even me but it's the only way to get through this, right now. "You can stay elsewhere, or anywhere, or whatever..."

Glen blinks rapidly. It looks like she is holding back tears. "If that's what you need... I understand. I will stay here, on the couch, and will be here to talk when you can. I don't want Mel. I just want to close that book and be honest about how I feel..." She steps toward me.

I step back, away from her. I am just holding on.

I nod at her numbly and turn away, willing myself not to look back at her. I will shatter completely if I do. I take a bottle of gin from the cupboard beside the fridge and an empty wine glass from the side of the sink and walk to the bedroom, locking the door firmly behind me.

Collapsing onto the bed, no tears come as reality sinks in its claws.

I'm still curled on the bed, drinking gin from a wine glass, some time later when I hear a soft knock. "Liz. Let's talk. I don't want this to be this way, to end this way. I can't see my life without you. I just need — needed — some space to sort this out. To come back to you. Please talk to me." Glen's muffled voice filters through the door. I clench my jaw, ignoring her.

Eventually I don't hear her anymore.

I wake early, confused for a minute by the unfamiliar shadows running across my... oh, not mine... Glen's... Glen and Melanie's ceiling.

Reality comes crashing back — Glen is sleeping just outside the door, on a ratty couch? At Melanie's? Somewhere else? But, anyway, not here in bed with me.

The change happened without an argument. No fight, no... nothing. One day we are waking up naked and curled together in a small bed in a flat above a pub near Norwich, chatting about our upcoming day or our next trip to London or, a book we want to read, and then, the next day, she needs to move away for work, for a job, for some career changes, which turns out was really just some space, for... what... some time to deal with... what? What did she need time to deal with? Her feelings for Melanie? Her feelings for me? Which was she trying to resolve?

Taking a deep breath, I snip my thoughts off. I won't find any answers.

I walk out of the bedroom groggy and puffy-eyed. Glen is not here. I don't want to think about where she must be, but I do. She's probably already waking up in Melanie's arms. I don't even bother to try not to think about all the clichés 'what goes around comes around', 'you reap what you sow, 'what's good for the goose'... yeah, possibly I should have known better.

Probably I should have known better.

Some relationships simply aren't meant to be real. No matter how much we fool ourselves into thinking they could be. No matter how much we might want them to be.

And all I can do now is keep moving, and find the train station, and find a place to go, and hope time, and maybe more gin, will eventually numb this exquisite sadness, this desperate weight in my center, crushing me.

I pour myself the rest of the gin.

On my way back to the train station I stop at the liquor store — which I should call the off-license, here in England, but, I suppose, what I call things doesn't matter anymore, now — I saw on my walk here.

The rain starts just after I make it through the train station doors so at least I am not drenched as I watch the British landscape speed by through the train windows on the four hour trip back to Norwich. I would wonder where I lost my way, where the joy in my life — where the possibility of a happy future — disappeared to, but I am not certain I ever held this joy — this possibility — long enough for it to qualify as having disappeared.

Spiraling

STRANGER THINGS HAPPEN

THE MORNING after arriving on Sierra's doorstep, I awaken with a pounding headache. It has only been a day, maybe two now — time seems a bit fuzzy in my head — since I packed my two bags and walked out of the Crown. Glen had phoned the morning I left and the pub owner was openly surprised that I wouldn't take the call. And he was even more shocked when, 45 minutes later, I wheeled my two bags down the drive to wait at the corner of the village green for the bus to Norwich where I caught a train to London.

Shuffling into the kitchen, I find Sierra eating cereal at the kitchen counter with her nose buried in home improvement magazine.

"You look like hell," she comments without even looking up.

I brace myself against the counter, rubbing my eyes. "Gee, thanks."

Sierra slaps the magazine down on the counter top. "Look, I said you could crash here for a few days but don't expect me to hold your hand through moping over Glen, okay?" She meets my eyes, "And, if I am going to be truly honest about it, I don't really have any sympathy for you, seems pretty much identical to the screwing-over you did to me in Toronto, huh. What's that called? Ch'anié ... anyway, she's not worth it."

Her bluntness is so true it doesn't even sting. She is right and she shouldn't have any sympathy for me, and I shouldn't be so sorry for myself. "You're right. I just need to sort myself out. Maybe find a job," at her look, I add, "and an apartment."

She eyes me skeptically, "Yeah, well. That'll be easier said than done without a work visa, and London is super expensive. You thought Toronto was bad? It is so much more expensive here... anyway, you might find a pub job though, they do hire foreigners. Usually under the table. And our accents actually are assets, here..."

"I will make it work," I insist. I know it's bravado and if I couldn't make it work at home, where I had employment options, there isn't much chance I can make it here, where there are none. Inside, I just want to curl up on the couch and cry at my lost life.

But that isn't an option.

"Sure. Yeah, maybe you will," Sierra grins. "Anyway, how about we go out tonight, see what we can find out there. Who knows, maybe your one-true-love is at a bar in King's Cross! Or, maybe mine is!" She guffaws.

* * *

It's Saturday night, and my five-day anniversary staying with Sierra, and she has dragged me out, again, to her favorite women's pub. But if I am honest with myself, there is no dragging involved. I need the distraction that drinking gives me. And the obliteration. And doing this in Sierra's flat during the day just feels weird.

I have stopped in at the pubs within walking distance of Sierra's but have had no luck finding anyone who can hire me under the table, this time of year. They all tell me the same thing — they are busier, and would need the extra staff in the summer, but that is months away, and useless to me.

Sierra claims a small table in the corner and we settle in with pints of the house draft. I don't like British beer any more than I like Canadian beer, but Sierra bought it, and it is easier to sneak drinks from my own — Canadian — version of a pint, with my preferred contents — gin — when I have a socially acceptable beverage sitting in front of me.

We people watch, in silence, and drink, in silence. Both of us are very good at that: the silence, and the drinking.

Eventually I notice a blond leaning against the bar, chatting with a handful of other women gathered around her. She throws her head back, laughing. My stomach flips. She reminds me of Toni, that first night in the Pool Queue, playing pool and drinking and flirting... back before I had fully experienced the reality of life.

When our eyes meet from across the room, the blond smiles widely and raises her drink in greeting. I can't help smiling in return before glancing away. I feel my cheeks warming.

Sierra notices my reaction and nudges me slyly, "Go on then, give that sweet thing something Canadian to talk about. And get us some refills." She waggles her eyebrows and makes a shooing motion.

Heart racing, I saunter over to order another round. I pretend to focus on the bartender pulling the pints for Sierra and I. But I check out the blond, casually... subtly.

Or maybe not so subtly. She steps around the woman standing between us and stands only a foot away. Her eyes are a piercing blue and she grins playfully.

"I'm Jen," she offers with an Irish lilt, holding out a hand. When I introduce myself and take her hand, the touch lances a rush through me.

A rush that almost feels like shame.

* * *

By last call, Jen has convinced me to join their after-party back at her flat around the corner.

She reminds me so much of Toni. Of a past when I still had

choices ahead of me, before I fucked everything up by coming here to England, by moving to Toronto even, perhaps.

And, I have to admit to myself, the prospect of going back to that state of anticipation excites me. The anticipation of going to bed with some hot blond and drinking and fucking and drinking some more. This will make me feel alive again, especially after this past week of self-numbing drifting. After these past weeks... after these past months...

As we stumble out into the street arm in arm, a combination of giddiness, recklessness, and liquid courage spur me onward. Sierra has long disappeared. I don't know when, or to where. Jen's smile promises distraction, even if only for a little while, and I truly have nothing to lose.

The after-party carries on with a small group of women and music and chatting and more drinking well into the early hours.

I lose myself in the chatter and the alcohol, and, eventually, in Jen's lips.

Reason is drowned.

* * *

It is nearly sunrise when a muffled thud jolts me awake.

My head still spins with the alcohol.

I am disoriented. I look around the strange room. At the naked blond stranger lying on top of the covers on a strange bed. At myself, lying beside her.

I don't see my clothes.

I wander into the living area and see a woman sleeping on the couch. She is wearing wooly socks, and nothing else. She does not stir as I walk past her.

I find my clothes on the floor in the bathroom. They are semi-neatly piled in front of a closed laundry hamper.

I look at my reflection in the mirror.

What am I doing?

I rub my face. This isn't me. This cannot be me. I cannot be this.

Panic grips me. I've let things spiral too far. I am clinging to nothing.

I cling to nothing. My life is a mess.

I need to own my mess. I need to own my life. This is not working.

Sliding into my clothes, I slip quietly out into the sunrise.

By the time I make it to Sierra's, I think I am mostly sober. I do not have a key, so I knock for several minutes before she opens the door and stares at me. "Fuck, can't you stay wherever you were. It's like, what, 7 am?"

"8. It's after 8 now."

Wordlessly, she steps back and lets me in.

* * *

Sierra places a cup of black coffee on the coffee table in front of where I am half-asleep on the couch. "You gotta pull this together. This isn't working."

I nod. And force myself to sit up and pick up the coffee. "I will."

She just stares at me.

"I know... I know... I will. I am."

She doesn't offer any words of comfort, or wisdom, or, actually speak to me at all. She just watches me, stony-faced.

"Sierra?" Her stony silence is weird.

She stares at me for another minute. "You've got until the end of the week. Then you're gone," she informs me coldly. "This is enough bullshit. You need to grow the fuck up."

I tell myself I'll pull myself together. I tell her this too.

. . .

But each day bleeds into the next until the week blurs seamlessly to its end.

The sound of running water wakes me from my restless dreams. Instinctively, I reach for the bottle I had left on the coffee table, only to find it missing.

Sierra stands by the breakfast bar, empty whiskey bottle in hand. "Time's up. Pack your things," she orders. "You're out. Now. This morning. Out this morning, by noon, or I will, literally, toss your stuff in the yard and throw you out after it."

I try to think up excuses.

But I come up empty. I am drowned.

She's right to kick me out — I'm so lost. I am so drowned. I need to come up for breath. I watch as she drops my empty whiskey bottle into the recycle bin.

The weird relief that surges through me scares me.

I know I have nowhere else to turn.

Shame burns my cheeks as I dial her number from Sierra's land line, while Sierra waits in the kitchen for me to figure out how I am going to leave. The when is already determined — now. And the to-where isn't of concern, to Sierra anyway.

Toni answers on the second ring.

"Hi. Toni?"

When she realizes it's me, I imagine I hear suspicion in her voice.

"Liz? What do you want? Do you know what time it is?"

I do know what time it is. 6:40 a.m. in Toronto. 11:40 a.m. here in London. My time is up. I have 20 minutes before Sierra will throw my bags out the front door and I believe her threat to do the same with me.

Memories of my last conversation with Toni spin in my head. I know she *told me so*.

I wonder if she will tell me that now... that she told me so. She would not be wrong to do so.

I swallow my pride. "Toni. Uh. I, uh, need help. Is there any way you would loan me money for a plane ticket home?"

Silence stretches. My shame makes me hot.

"You've finally hit rock bottom?"

I wince. But I don't speak. I don't have any other options.

"Where are you?"

As if she didn't know.

But, maybe she doesn't.

"I'm in England."

"Oh my God. I knew that English girl would chew you up. What are you doing in England?... well, I know *what* you're doing there, I mean, why do you need air fare to come home?"

"Toni. It doesn't matter. I will pay you back. I just need to get home."

"And, then what?"

Hot tears choke me. I grasp for any shreds of dignity I can find. "Toni..."

A long breath echoes down the line before she replies. "Alright. I'll transfer you the fare."

Sierra lets me make one more very short phone call.

I leave Sierra's with a few minutes to spare and wheel my two bags the four blocks to the subway which will take me to Heathrow where I am hopeful I can get a standby seat on an early morning flight. I do not stop at either of the two off-licences I pass.

I decline to drink while I wait the nearly 16 hours in the airport until I can board my flight.

I decline to drink on the plane. I watch the sun's orange glimmering above the clouds until I fall asleep with my head resting against the window.

Out of Rocks

I WAIT in the sunshine beaming in through the large windows to collect my luggage. The heat of it warms me, from the outside in. Logically, I know I can't feel the earth of Canada under my feet, and Toronto cannot be my home, but... the cold of logic melts in the warmth from the sun beaming in on me.

My entire collection of belongings spins around on a carousel in an airport in Toronto on a bright and sunny late Monday morning. My whole world in two bags. I try to force myself to see this as a positive thing, an anti-material fresh start to a new life. But an aching loneliness threatens to overwhelm me. I blame it on the lack of sleep and start hauling my two bags on their cheap built-in wheels through customs and down the escalator to... home...

When I come out through the sealed security doors to the general arrivals area, I see Cherry standing there. She is waiting outside the arrivals chute, holding a sign that reads "Return to me and all will be well" written along the top edge of a pencil replication of one of Cherry's Sappho paintings.

A warmth like the one I felt standing in the sunshine coming through the windows at the carousel spreads through me, outward this time — from my middle, out through my limbs. It melts a rock I didn't realize was sitting deep inside me. A sense of relief infuses me.

Cherry welcomes my hug. And she holds me back, in a long hug. A firm one. Then we separate and turn toward the exit.

"Remember that conversation we had, way back in the fall, about summer plans?"

Cherry nods.

"I don't have any, at all, now," I laugh.

She laughs with me and sticks her hand into the pull handle of the bag I am pulling with my right hand. I let the warmth of her skin rest against mine for a moment, before I remove my hand and let her take the bag.

We walk side by side. "I kicked Herbie out. One too many nights with the guys and a little too much aggression. I don't need that..."

She wheels one bag, shifting it over to her right hand.

I wheel one bag, with my left.

She takes my hand in the middle. "I have the car. Let's go to campus right now. You can meet with the department head and find out what your options are. They might have something you can do over the summer semester, to get you back on track."

She squeezes my hand gently. "And, you can stay with me. On the couch!" she adds hastily, with a giggle.

I am positive I hear her say "for now, anyway," but a loud-speaker announcing a license plate of a car that is illegally parked drowns out her voice.

I squeeze her hand back as the sliding doors let us out into my new world.

tell I didn't notice, was sitting deep inside me. A sense of relief
infuses me.

Come, we both see our Fate. And she holds me back in a long
hug. Then one. Then we separate and turn toward the...

"I remember that conversation we had. You had made me talk
about unimportant things."

Oh my aching...

"I don't have time at all now," I laugh.

She laughs with me and offers her hand into the pull handle of
the bag. I am pulling with my right hand, I let the weight of my
skin rest against mine for a moment. I don't remove my hand and
let her take the bag.

"We won't do it, due. Then? Here's me sure. One too many
nights on the ground a little to much depression, I don't need
that."

She whistles one big shrug, it over to her right hand.

I wheel the bag, with I pylon.

She takes my hand in the middle. M last this can. Let's go to
Japan right now. You can meet with the department head and
find out what your options are. They might have something you
can do over the summer, endeavor, to get you back on track.

She squeezes my hand gently. And you can stay with me. On
the couch," she adds hastily, with a giggle.

"I am trying. I breathe in," I... "I don't
appear important a little time place of a car that I illegally parked
down near her voice.

Suzan Digh is from Prince Edward Island, Canada and currently lives with her wife in New Brunswick. Suzan has several queer poetic-form books — on very dark topics — already in print.

On the Rocks is her first published prose-form novel. Her second prose-form novel (literary fiction) is due to be released in late spring 2025, and she is currently working on a lesbian detective series.

Suzan has been out of the closet her entire adult life and appreciates that she lives in a place and time that has allowed this. She hopes that the world stays the course and that each and every LGBTQ+ person can find their own place to be safe and loved.

Also by Suzan Digh

Out in the Dark

Shattered Remnants

Puss & Cunt, a poetic true love story

Mad (adj: angry, insane)

www.ingramcontent.com/pod-product-compliance
Lightning Source LLC
Chambersburg PA
CBHW010801310726
48974CB00006B/926